"Full Impulse, Capt
Janeway commanded.

At the conn, Lieutenant Stadi obeyed, the ship humming with power as she brought it about. At Ops, Ensign Kim remained glued to his readouts. "The tetryon wave will intercept us in twenty seconds . . ." he began.

"Can we go to warp?" Janeway asked Stadi, knowing the answer.

Stadi shook her head. "Not until we clear the plasma field, Captain."

". . . eight seconds," Ensign Kim continued.

". . . five . . .

". . . four . . .

". . . three . . ."

"Brace for impact!" Janeway shouted. The intercom spread her voice through the ship just as the hand of God took the *Voyager* in its grip and flung it into the void. . . .

Look for STAR TREK Fiction from Pocket Books

Star Trek: The Original Series

Star Trek: The Next Generation

Star Trek: Deep Space Nine

Star Trek: Voyager

STAR TREK VOYAGER™

CARETAKER

A Novel by L.A. GRAF

Based on a script by Michael Piller & Jeri Taylor
Story by Rick Berman & Michael Piller & Jeri Taylor

POCKET BOOKS
New York   London   Toronto   Sydney   Tokyo   Singapore

An *Original* Publication of POCKET BOOKS

POCKET BOOKS, a division of Simon & Schuster Inc.
1230 Avenue of the Americas, New York, NY 10020

This book is published by Pocket Books, a division of Simon & Schuster Inc., under exclusive license from Paramount Pictures.

ISBN: 0-671-51914-X

First Pocket Books printing February 1995

10 9 8 7 6 5

POCKET BOOKS and colophon are registered trademarks of Simon & Schuster Inc.

Cover photo by Julie Dennis
Cover photo copyright © 1995 by Paramount Pictures

Printed in the U.S.A.

Acknowledgments

Special thanks to Dennis Bailey and Arne Starr
for services above and beyond the call of duty.
You guys are aces!

A ROAR OF SCARLET LIGHT BLASTED THROUGH THE TINY spaceship's bridge, and alarms screamed as if in surprise as the deadly tremor of a direct hit went rattling off down the ship's already battered frame. Chakotay wound his ankles more securely around the base of his pilot's chair to keep from being pitched to the deck, then tapped a rapid sequence on the panel without looking back to see how the rest of his crew fared. If he looked, he would have to go to them, and there was no place for that just now. *A time to fight, a time to mourn,* he tried to console himself. Chakotay didn't remember anymore what noble figure in his people's past had first said that. He wondered if that old Indian had ever faced anything quite like this.

The ship's engines stuttered, then barked suddenly into life to spiral them off at an oblique vector.

Another blast of light shattered across the viewscreen dominating Chakotay's vision, and this time he had to grab the console itself as the ship bucked out from under him.

"Direct hit." Tuvok sat his station as easily as he would have on any planetbound installation— unperturbed, unshaken. Skin and hair the color of polished walnut blended the Vulcan into near invisibility under the ship's unnatural darkness. It wasn't as if Chakotay would have seen anything interesting in Tuvok's expression, anyway—Vulcan discipline rendered the alien's face as emotionless as his voice, making him a steady (if uninspiring) companion in such fights. "Shields at sixty percent . . ."

"A fuel line has ruptured," Torres's voice added to the litany from somewhere out of Chakotay's sight. "Attempting to compensate . . ."

This time, Chakotay felt the belly of his ship split open under the force of a torpedo strike too distant to count as a hit, too near to be ignored as a miss. Even so, he couldn't help smiling, just a little, at Torres's roar of frustration as she kicked and pummeled her panel at the back of the craft.

"Dammit!" Her voice fairly dripped with the Klingon anger she'd unwillingly inherited from her mother's contribution to her genes. "We're barely maintaining impulse. I can't get any more out of it—"

Chakotay sensed the next shot coming, easing their craft into a turn he hoped would be fast enough without blowing out their damaged engines. "Be creative."

Torres exploded a Latino curse in his direction. "How am I supposed to be 'creative' with a thirty-nine-year-old rebuilt engine—"

"Maquis ship!" The gray, leathern face of a mature Cardassian flashed onto the viewscreen, blotting out the starscape. "This is Gul Evek of the Cardassian Fourth Order. Cut your engines and prepare to sur—"

Chakotay interrupted his piloting only long enough to close the comm channel with the heel of his hand.

"Initiating evasive pattern omega . . ." Something let loose with a crash and *whoosh!* of flame. Chakotay ducked his head away from the rain of sparks that singed his close-cropped hair, and keyed the sequence. "Mark!"

The ship jerked like a rabid dog, then started to run.

When Chakotay had been a boy only just taking the first steps into what would become the journey of his manhood, he'd traveled out west with his father and uncle, stayed awake for almost three days in woods so very like where his ancestors used to live, and chanted to keep himself brave as his father and uncle tattooed the first lines into his virgin face. *Remember,* they had told him, *what you are made of. Every time you look in a mirror, remember that less than five hundred years ago, the grandfathers who preserved these marks for you stood in woodlands light-years away with their knives and arrows, throwing sticks and shields, and fought a wave of ignorant invaders so that you and other children like you could be born and taught and tattooed in the way of our people for centuries to come.* What his father didn't talk about was how, despite the mighty battles waged by Chakotay's forefathers, those ignorant invaders had taken the land, relocated the families, and done everything possible to make sure the prayers and language and tattoos didn't survive, all in the name of what they believed was virtuous and right. But Chakotay had known all that already. He'd known it from history tapes and museum exhibits—known that the tolerance and freedom he and his people enjoyed on their fertile colony world had not always existed. And he had been fiercely grateful to everyone who had fought to preserve this life for him.

Yet now, hundreds of thousands of miles away from the planet his ancestors had called home, Chakotay found himself allied with a band of proud colonists who wanted only to save their homes and families and ways of life, just like those Indians on long-ago Earth. No matter how just and necessary the Federation believed its treaty with the Cardassians—no matter how many times some admiral claimed they were sorry to abandon the border colonies to the uncertainties of life under Cardassian rule—Chakotay couldn't make himself believe this situation was any different than a hundred other stories where the dominant culture imposed its will on peoples who hadn't the power to turn back the tide.

He'd be damned if he let that happen again here. If nothing else, he owed it to his grandfathers.

Something shoved at the ship from behind, and Tuvok reported evenly, "Shields at fifty percent."

Damn. Chakotay twisted a look at Torres without lifting his hands from the controls. "I need more power."

"Okay . . ." She blinked, her thick brow ridge wrinkling as the fluid mind beneath her black mane darted through more engineering options than Chakotay even knew. "Okay," she said again, suddenly, "take the weapons off-line. We'll transfer all power to the engines."

Tuvok lifted his head with a politely arched eyebrow. "Considering the circumstances, I'd question that proposal at this time."

"What does it matter?" Torres shot back acidly. "We're not making a dent in their shields anyway." She returned Chakotay's unhappy sigh with a battle stare that, even coming from a half-Klingon, could have melted pure deuterium. "You wanted 'creative.'"

Not "wanted"—didn't have a choice. There really was a difference.

5

Chakotay turned back to his panels as another blast from the Cardassian ship burned into their shields. "Tuvok, shut down all the phaser banks." He flicked a hopeful look at Torres. "If you can give me another thirty seconds at full impulse, I'll get us into the Badlands." The best of all possible options, and not a good one, at that.

"Phasers off-line," Tuvok reported. He sounded as unhappy as a Vulcan ever did.

"Throw the last photons at them," Chakotay told him, his mind already racing ahead in an effort to construct a preliminary course through the Badlands' plasma storm maze. "Then give me the power from the torpedo system. . . ."

"Acknowledged." Tuvok primed the warheads with a flick of his hand. "Firing photons."

A bark of percussive thunder, and the little ship jolted at every launch. The answering flash and rumble of the torpedoes slamming against those impenetrable Cardassian shields only encouraged Chakotay a little.

"Are you reading any plasma storms ahead?" he asked Tuvok.

"One," the Vulcan replied. "Coordinates one-seven-one mark four-three."

Chakotay nodded once, shortly. "That's where I'm going . . ."

The ship responded to his commands like a brain-dead mammoth—slowly, stumbling. *We've got to get out of here,* Chakotay thought, feeling weirdly as if that urgency had only just occurred to him. As they dropped down and starboard, a surge of unseen energy splashed against the ship like a careless wave. The absence of curses and alarms told him it hadn't been a Cardassian torpedo.

"Plasma storm density increasing by fourteen percent . . ." Tuvok's dark eyes stayed riveted to his sensors. ". . . twenty . . . twenty-five . . ."

Chakotay didn't need the Vulcan's recitation to feel the growing fury in the space distortion. It was just what he had hoped for. "Hold on!"

The crash of the storm swallowing them whole rivaled any blast from the Cardassian warship, but it was a welcome, familiar violence that lifted the crushing dread from Chakotay's heart even as it battered his tiny craft. Thrashing flares of electromagnetic fire writhed across the viewscreen, whipping their damaged shields like living tentacles as plasma rocked and shook and pitched the Maquis ship in warning of what they would face should they stray too close to the heart of that fury. It was a power Chakotay already respected well, and one he didn't plan to abuse. Weaving carefully between the grasping tendrils, he counted the seconds since the Cardassians last opened fire on them, and smiled.

As if aware of Chakotay's thoughts, Tuvok volunteered from the weapons station, "The Cardassian ship is not reducing power. They're following us in."

Chakotay aimed them neatly through a tear in the plasma hardly large enough to take them. "Gul Evek must be feeling daring today."

Tuvok inset the video from his sensors to the edge of the main viewscreen, granting Chakotay the privilege of watching without interrupting the pilot's work. It was worth having the chance to sneak a look, Chakotay admitted. The huge Cardassian vessel twisted and jumped as plasma discharge racked it from all sides. Chakotay recognized their pattern—a crude attempt to follow the path sketched out by the Maquis ship on its way into the maelstrom. He couldn't wait to see what happened when they tried to thread that plasma needle he'd just squeezed through.

Evek's ship wrenched suddenly sideways—to avoid the skirl of fire biting at its belly, Chakotay supposed—only to have its upflung nacelle engulfed in a hungry tentacle that swelled all too quickly into a searing blast of light and spinning debris. He caught the briefest glimpse of the warship as it tumbled over itself and off visual, trailing glowing destruction behind it.

"They're sending out a distress signal on all Cardassian frequencies," Tuvok reported. Which meant most of them were still alive. Too bad.

Torres snorted and thumped a fist on her panel in pleasure. "Evek was a fool to take a ship that size into the Badlands."

"Anyone's a fool to take a ship into the Badlands," Chakotay reminded her, and she rewarded him with one of her rare, sharp-toothed smiles and a rude gesture with one hand.

Still grinning, Chakotay passed his gaze over Tuvok on his way to returning all attention to his console. "Can you plot a course through these plasma fields, Mr. Tuvok?" It would be nice to have something to work from other than the seat of his pants, not to mention nice to let the computer do some of the work for a while.

"The storm activity is typically widespread in this vicinity." Tuvok fell silent as he swept their surroundings with whatever sensors the Cardassians had left them. "I can plot a course," he decided at last, "but I am afraid it will require an indirect route."

Chakotay shrugged, enjoying the luxury. "We're in no hurry."

Tuvok didn't seem to appreciate the dry humor —after all, with no warp drive and damn little impulse, there wasn't much hurrying they could do—but Chakotay had learned to enjoy the opportunities for humor made available by a Vulcan's literal mind. Humor was something hard to come by in the Maquis these days.

Chakotay waited for the telltales on his panel to blink acceptance of the computer's control, then pushed away from the console to climb stiffly to his feet. Muscles all down his back twinged in none-too-gentle reminder of the hours he'd spent hunched in the tiny pilot's seat. He pulled his face into a grimace and stretched until his hands brushed the ceiling. Even with the ship still jumping and rumbling through the trails of plasma discharge, it felt good to be standing. He was getting too old for this kind of cat-and-mousing every day.

Torres remained glued to her station, calling damage reports and instructions to other parts of the ship while trying to sort out a snake's coil of cables from around her feet. Other crew had appeared from nowhere, the noise of their cleanup a happy, relieved sound after the grim silence of the long battle. This was hard on them, Chakotay knew. So many colonists came into the Maquis because they wanted to save themselves and their families, not because they wanted to die. Coming so close in a claustrophobic rattrap that had been smuggled into the Demilitarized Zone only months before by an overpriced Ferengi marketeer was enough to make even the most stalwart revolutionary question the wisdom of his fight. He expected to lose a good quarter of the crew once they set down for repairs among the Terikof Belt planetoids. Like always.

He clapped Torres on the back as he slipped past her, earning a startled jerk of her head in reply. He met her uncertain frown with a smile and an upraised thumb, appreciative of her good work over the last few hours, knowing how wrong it would be to try and tell her so. She grunted, flushing that distinct shade of umber that no full Klingon would ever exhibit, and turned back to her panel with a terse nod. Satisfied that she'd understood the compliment, even if it made her uncomfortable, Chakotay moved wearily toward the back of the command center to find the source of the ribbon of smoke that was steadily pooling in the struts overhead.

"I've heard Starfleet's commissioned a new Intrepid-class ship," Torres remarked suddenly. As though she knew she ought to say something in response to Chakotay's communication, but didn't know quite what. "With the bioneural circuitry to maneuver through plasma storms . . ." she added.

The smoke was spilling out of a grate beneath the atmosphere controls, weirdly lit from inside by both emergency flashers and loose flame. Chakotay pulled the grate open with a great puff of sooty air, and knelt to reach under the damaged panel. "We'll find a new place to hide," he remarked to Torres.

She was silent for a moment, and he used that time to find the trigger for the automatic fire controls and force it into the Active position with his thumb. Halon swirled around him in a chilling blast, and he jerked his arm back into the open to let the gas do its work.

"You ever think about what'll happen if they catch us?" Torres asked as he was settling the grate back into its tracks. The controls reported that function had been marginalized, but nothing was in danger of failing.

Chakotay added replacement of the atmospherics to the mental checklist of impossible repairs he already intended to hand the technicians at the hideout, and turned to decide which hopeless task to take up next. "My great-grandfather had a *poktoy*," he said to Torres as he prowled between the panels. At her dubious scowl, he smiled and clarified, "A saying, that he passed on to my grandfather, who passed it to my father, who passed it to me. *'Coya anochta zab.'*" The reclamation system had been fused in one of the countless torpedo hits, too ruined for him to even read the controls. He abandoned it, and moved on. " 'Don't look back.' "

Torres almost smiled, and Chakotay had to return her flash of grim humor when he considered how appropriate those words were to most of their battles anymore. *Take it where you can get it,* he chided himself. *Humor is hard to come by, remember?* Small wonder why.

"Curious . . ."

Tuvok's voice floated up from the weapons console as though the Vulcan didn't even realize he'd spoken. Chakotay watched as long, dark hands played across the controls, trying to recapture something no one but a Vulcan would probably even have seen.

Apparently satisfied with what he found, Tuvok lifted an eyebrow and traced a series of readings with his eyes. "We have just passed through some kind of coherent tetryon beam."

Chakotay's heart thumped against his lungs. *If the Cardassians have some new weaponry . . .* He shook the thought away, unwilling to think of that just now. "Source?" he asked as he climbed his way back to the front of the bridge.

Tuvok consulted his readings once more. "Unknown." As Chakotay squeezed in behind him, Torres as close on his heels as she could be without actually touching him, the Vulcan pointed to something incomprehensible among his readouts. "Now there appears to be a massive displacement wave moving toward us."

Chakotay shot a look out the viewscreen, seeing nothing but plasma turmoil, then turned in frustration to the swarm of scientific figures and the blur of formless white steadily obscuring them as it flowed onto the screen. "Another storm?"

Tuvok shook his head. "It is not a plasma phenomenon. The computer is unable to identify it."

"Put it onscreen."

The plasma storm swirling and raging beyond the forward viewscreen rippled and bled, peeling away from itself as the image projected there shifted to a new angle off the rear of the little craft. Chakotay felt his throat tighten at the thick wall of coruscating destruction that chewed its way through the storm behind them.

"At current speeds," Tuvok reported placidly, "it is going to intercept us in less than thirty seconds."

And eat us alive. Chakotay swung away from the

weapons console to throw himself at the helm. "Anything left in those impulse generators, B'Elanna?" he called back to Torres as he slipped into the seat.

She already struggled with her damaged equipment, growling profanities at whatever her console told her. "We'll find out."

"It is still exceeding our speed," Tuvok interjected.

Chakotay didn't bother acknowledging. "Maximum power."

"You've got it," Torres replied.

But even as the craft lurched forward, he could feel the wave roiling toward them—like the stinging kiss of too-near fire, or the brush of an owl's wing as it dove toward someone's death in the night. *Not like this,* he prayed. *After everything we've been through, everything we've dreamed, please don't let us lose our lives like this!*

"The wave is continuing to accelerate." A rhythmic pinging underscored the Vulcan's deep voice as he counted off the seconds. "It will intercept us in eight seconds . . . five . . ."

Chakotay locked his feet around the chair's base again, his hands frozen on the panel, but unable to command any more speed from the ruined craft.

Not like this!

Sirens first, then screams, then the groan of tortured metal. He clenched his teeth, wished he could close his ears, damning the Federation for their ill-thought treaty, damning the Cardassians for chasing them in here, damning whatever explosion of nature now chased them, slammed them, clawed them, ripped them open like a rotten fish until the ship streamed its viscera a molecule wide into forever, into nowhere, into nothing—

Not like this not like this not like—!

CHAPTER

1

"CAPTAIN KATHRYN JANEWAY, THIS IS AUCKLAND Control. You are now cleared for landing at Federation Penal Settlement, Landing Pad Three."

Blinking her attention back to the present, Janeway reached for the comm toggle with no conscious decision to do so, directed by instinct and habit when fatigue wouldn't allow her much else to go on. "Janeway to Auckland Control, roger. Landing approach at one-three-one-mark-seven."

"Roger, Janeway," the bright New Zealand voice on the other end of the channel replied. "Enjoy your stay."

She set about the business of guiding her slim shuttle past the island's rugged mountains without dignifying the Kiwi's sarcasm with a reply.

The sheer greenness of New Zealand's North Island reached up through the clean ocean air to hug Janeway's heart with warmth. As temperate and mild a place as San Francisco was, it was still penciled on the coastline in shades of minty gray. Fog and rock and juniper, not mountains, trees and snow like the wild panorama galloping below her. It seemed a shame to waste such beauty on felons. No matter how hard she tried to tell herself that even criminals were humans, deserving of certain dignities and rights, she couldn't quite divest herself of the belief that incarceration for serious crimes should be unpleasant and dull. Why take up land that could be added to New Zealand's magnificent National Parks system when Alcatraz still crouched in the midst of San Francisco Bay, useless to everybody but tourists and seagulls? After all, the felons sunning themselves on Auckland's beaches right now should be contemplating how badly they never wanted to end up in prison again, not budgeting time for another stint here as though planning some kind of expense-paid vacation.

That isn't fair, she scolded herself. *They make them work here, and rehabilitation facilities like this enjoy a much higher success rate than the old-style punishment systems.* Still, a deeper part of her chafed at the idea of cutting anyone else slack when she allowed so little room for error in herself.

The penal settlement accepted her clearance code without question, and she allowed the penitentiary's flight computer to take the shuttle's controls for the final approach and touchdown. It felt good, actually, to sit back—even for a few minutes—and rest her brain from the endless onslaught of decisions it had been forced to make over the last few days. Mark, bless him, had been as supportive as a civilian lovemate could be, never questioning the hours she spent away from him (even when they were together), never demanding that he be more important than the things that Starfleet threw in front of her to reconcile. Even when Bear had gotten sick, poor angel, Mark had taken her to the vet without being asked, letting the big dog ride the whole way with her head in his lap, even though it meant dun-colored hairs on his trousers for the rest of the week. Janeway knew how much he hated dealing with dog hair.

Why does everything come down at once? she asked herself with a weary sigh. A part of her still hadn't forgiven herself for handing Bear over to the kennel this morning, still with no idea why the dog had suddenly swelled by nearly seven kilos and fallen into a persistent lazy torpor. *If anything happens to her while I'm gone, I'll hate myself.*

And if anything happened to her wayward security officer because she couldn't get *Voyager* out of port just one day earlier, she'd hate herself for that, too. There was just no way of winning this one.

The comp at the main gate was expecting her. Walking across the bright, open field separating the two aircraft permanently assigned to this settlement from the actual facility that housed the detainees, Janeway marveled again at the sweetness of the air, the beauty of the cerulean sky. *I need a vacation,* she decided. Bad timing, that. She passed inside the gates on voiceprint and retinal scan only, and wasn't even past the second barrier before the security system informed her, "Detainee Thomas E. Paris is in the motor fleet repair bay. Would you like a security car to take you there?"

"No," she told it. "I'd rather walk."

It neither thanked her nor signed off; she left the gate behind without caring.

For all that they couldn't have many visitors to the penal settlement, the detainees she passed didn't seem particularly interested in her arrival. She couldn't imagine that they'd known she'd be coming. More likely, the arrival of a Starfleet officer meant nothing but trouble for somebody within this facility, and nobody particularly wanted to be that somebody. Just as well. She wasn't in the mood to talk right now, least of all to anyone who couldn't figure out how to keep *themselves* out of serious trouble, much less rescue a stubborn friend from the fire.

She found Paris on the pavement outside the repair bay, the only detainee in sight—and even then, only half so. His upper torso was hidden beneath some long, squat piece of equipment with a power coil the size of an asteroid, his shirt flung carelessly over the machine's control console and a plasma welder flashing arrhythmically from somewhere out of sight beside him. Janeway took in the details of his assignment—the level of equipment he was allowed to use without supervision, the apparent mobility of the machine he worked to repair—and noted to herself that even the electronic anklet locked to his right foot couldn't stop him from fleeing the island if he chose to at this moment. It could find him, wherever he fled, but it couldn't prevent his escape. The fact that he was still here said something about either his commitment to his own rehab, or his intelligence. She didn't know him well enough yet to determine which it was.

Taking a breath to clear her thoughts and school the dislike from her features, she clasped her hands loosely behind her back. "Tom Paris?" She summoned him as though only just coming up on the scene, seeing no need to surrender any advantage she didn't have to. Not to this kid. Not knowing the kind of stock he came from.

The flailing light under the machinery's belly died abruptly, leaving a smear of darkness across her vision as an echo of its brightness. Paris pushed himself out from under with a smoothness that betrayed the gliding board he must have had in place under his back, and flicked up the visor that hid his eyes as though lifting an extremely chic and expensive pair of sunglasses. Sweat sheened down the middle of his chest and across the flat plane of his stomach, and Janeway noted that his pale skin glowed just a bit too pinkly below his collar line and above his cuffs. Not used to New Zealand's bright winter sun, then, and too proud to move himself inside when the daylight threatened to burn. That indicated a special type of stupidity, reserved for young men who felt they had something to prove but hadn't a clue what it was. Very like the description she'd been given before flying down to New Zealand, and not at all like his father.

"Kathryn Janeway," she identified herself. She didn't offer her hand, and he gave no sign that he expected it. "I served with your father on the *Al-Batani*. I wonder if we could go somewhere and talk."

An odd little smile that seemed to go deeper than it should ghosted onto his face at the mention of his father. Janeway wondered what sort of thoughts moved behind an expression like that. "About what?" Paris asked her, still stretched full-length on the gliding board.

"About a job we'd like you to do for us."

He laughed—a laugh as odd and light as his smile—and tossed a hand toward the machine above him. "I'm already doing a 'job,'" he explained with mock sincerity. "For the Federation."

Attitude looking for a place to happen. Janeway had been warned, but it didn't make her like it any more. Still, a dozen years of service had taught her well how to temper her tone and expression. "I've been told the Rehab Committee is very pleased with your work. They've given me their approval to discuss this matter with you."

Paris studied her with eyes that held a hint of an intellect far keener than his history implied. Then he shrugged, as though dismissing everything he'd just allowed himself to think, and bounced to his feet with an easy grace that spoke volumes about the training and life he'd known before this. He faced her with arms spread, that infuriating grin laid out between them like a shield. "Then I guess I'm yours."

Only if I decide I want you, Janeway thought back at him, her face as cool and stern as possible. *And then only if I decide I need you.* She didn't have time to waste on him otherwise.

A park. The damn penal facility had a park. Janeway walked with Paris between the full, green trees, seething at the lovely solitude of the place amid these people who seemed, by temperament, ill-suited to appreciate it. Still, it was Paris who slowed to pluck an errant scrap of plastic off the walkway—Paris who detoured them around a bob of oblivious pigeons so that their conversation wouldn't disrupt the birds. And, all the while, he undercut the notion of his own decency every time Janeway began to think there might be something more to this rebellious boy than anyone realized. If nothing else, he was certainly a complicated young man. She wasn't sure she wanted complicated for this delicate a mission.

"Your father taught me a great deal," she said when one of his self-deprecating slurs laid out an overlong silence between them. "I was his science officer during the Arias Expedition."

Paris nodded, thoughtfully. "You must be good. My father only accepts the best and the brightest." Surprisingly, the rancor she'd expected didn't surface in his voice. Perhaps the worst of it only reached inward instead of out.

She followed on the heels of his reasonability before it could crumble away. "I'm leaving on a mission to find a Maquis ship that disappeared in the Badlands a week ago."

"I wouldn't if I were you."

The easy certainty of his tone made it sound like he was commenting on the soccer scores, not a trek into the worst uncharted space. "Really?" she prompted dryly.

He nodded again, more seriously, and even dared stealing a direct look at her face, as if to make sure she was listening. "I've never seen a Federation starship that could maneuver through the plasma storms."

"You've never seen *Voyager*," she told him, and quietly enjoyed the flash of jealous curiosity that jumped into his eyes. "We'd like you to come along."

Bitter understanding supplanted whatever interest had started to get a foothold in his brain. "You'd like me to lead you to my former colleagues." He wasn't guessing, though she knew he meant it to sound that way, and the half-angry, half-mocking smile that seemed his constant companion finished the job of banishing her respect. "I was only with the Maquis a few weeks before I was captured, Captain. I don't know where most of their hiding places are."

"You know the territory better than anyone we've got." He had to know that was true.

Whether he believed it or not, he shrugged off Janeway's comment the way he might a drink offer during a long and boring dinner party. "What's so important about this particular Maquis ship?"

A fair enough question, considering Starfleet hadn't followed any of the other hit-and-run raiders so far into their own territory. "My chief of security was on board. Undercover. He was supposed to report in twice during the last six days." She blinked off an unwelcome memory of the night she'd spent sleepless, waiting for her trusted friend's last scheduled call. "He didn't."

Paris snorted at some personal joke she hadn't heard. "Maybe it's just your chief of security who's disappeared."

The possibility hurt, but . . . "Maybe."

She gave him a moment to study whatever thoughts her proposition awakened in him, eager to shake an answer out of him, leery of frightening him off when he was the only real chance they had. When she glanced away from the tower of distant mountains to see where his reflections had led him, she found Paris staring at her with surprising intensity. Their eyes met for just that instant, and he turned away with a mortified blush creeping up his cheeks toward his hairline.

Janeway discreetly averted her gaze, pretending not to notice.

"That ship was under the command of another former Starfleet officer named Chakotay," she said, giving him a chance to catch up with her conversation before forcing him into an answer. "I understand you knew him."

"That's right." He quirked a grin, as though remembering rowdy weekends at the Academy, or a wild first assignment with a brace of other young men.

Janeway watched him carefully. "The two of you didn't get along too well, I'm told."

He shrugged, laughing, and tossed his arms out as though absolving himself of all responsibility for anything this Chakotay might have claimed. "Chakotay would tell you he left Starfleet on principle," Paris explained. "To defend his home colony from the Cardassians." He folded both hands across his chest in beatific innocence. "I, on the other hand, was forced to resign. He considered me a mercenary—willing to fight for anyone who could pay my bar bills. Trouble is—" He shrugged again, grinning. "He was right."

He turned away from her, walking slowly and easily down a sun-dappled path that led nowhere, just like his life. "I have no problem helping you track down my 'friends' in the Maquis, Captain. All I need to know is—" He flicked her a look. "What's in it for me?"

It always comes down to that with your kind, she thought. Then, immediately, she had to admit that it wasn't the goodness of her own heart that had brought her here to barter Paris's freedom. Everyone was just a little bit selfish, each in his own way. People like Paris just made more of an art of it, that was all.

"You help us find that ship," Janeway told him. "We help you at your next outmate review."

"Uh-uh." Paris waggled a finger at her, picking his leg up between them to tap at the anklet. "I get the anklet off first. Then I help you."

Janeway had expected this—had arranged for it already, in fact. If the Rehab Committee wasn't going to let their prize delinquent go, there was no sense wasting time bartering with Paris. And if Paris was ready to agree to her terms, Janeway equally didn't want to waste time arguing with a slow-as-dirt committee about something as trivial as a detention anklet that wouldn't serve its function anyway once they shipped off Earth. Still, all she said to Paris was "I'll look into it."

He rolled his eyes as though it made no difference to him, and squinted up toward the mountains as though fascinated by their whiteness.

"Officially, you'd be a Starfleet observer during the mission."

"Observer?" True insult etched a frown into his young face. "Hell, I'm the best pilot you could have."

She shrugged, intentionally echoing him, and watched the fragile surface of his bravado crack and come apart again under the implied disinterest. "You'll be an observer," she said, more firmly. "When it's over, you're cut loose."

Paris attempted a wounded sigh. "The story of my life."

It took everything inside her not to turn her back on him and leave him here to rot in his government-paid paradise surrounded by all the rest of the losers he'd cast his lot with when he first blew off his duty more than a year before. Stepping up to him—so close he jerked a startled look at her and tried to back himself away—she took his chin in one hand and held him in place the way she would a disobedient twelve-year-old. The very childlike terror in his eyes only served to make him look even younger, even less deserving of this sacrifice or her trust.

"If a member of my crew gets hurt because you make a mistake," she told him, very softly, "you won't have to worry about an anklet, mister. I'll make sure you don't see daylight again."

Paris didn't say anything as Janeway glared at him to drive her point home, didn't say anything when she released him, didn't say anything when she turned to walk away.

Who knows? she thought. *Maybe he is trainable, after all.*

CHAPTER

2

THE SLENDER SPIRAL OF SPACE STATION *DEEP SPACE Nine* turned in graceful pirouette against the un-populated backdrop of open space. It made a strange yet lovely sight—unlike any other structure Starfleet recognized as an orbital space station, but still as pretty and functional as her alien architects could make her. If she had had anything beneath her to orbit, she might not even look so weirdly displaced, although Paris doubted that.

Somewhere within a few AUs of *Deep Space Nine's* northern elliptic, a scarred and war-battered world called Bajor supposedly marked the path originally followed by this wayward station. Paris remembered hearing rumblings two years ago about the stable wormhole accidentally discovered in this sector, and about DS9's consequent relocation to the mouth of that anomaly. He'd discounted it all as sensationalist newsnet drivel. *Shows what I know.* Slouching farther down in his seat, he braced his heels against the edge of his inactive copilot's helm and watched the station draw closer through the V of his upraised knees.

It felt odd, sitting again in a Starfleet shuttle without guards at either shoulder or manacles on his hands. The memory of that last flight—and his last few hours inside a Starfleet uniform—brought heat into his cheeks so painfully, he thought he'd cry. He fought off the impulse with the skill of much practice. No sense mourning the past. What's done is done, and you can't undo it, and if the last miserable year of his life didn't prove that, nothing else did. *Be thankful for whatever bit of reprieve you can buy,* he told himself. If, in his case, this amounted to little more than a sterile, rankless uniform, a token position under a hostile commander, and the chance to improve his status from imprisoned Starfleet traitor bum to simple free-ranging civilian bum, then it was already better than he knew he deserved.

It would have been nice to be the pilot who first slipped a starship through that wormhole, though.

Shifting his duffel to a more comfortable position across his lap, Paris slid a look toward the lieutenant who had quietly piloted them ever since they parted company with the larger crew transport seven hours ago. She was small and pleasantly trim, like most Betazoid women Paris had seen, with the same high brow and huge, chocolate eyes that had slain human men since their races first crossed paths. He'd tried talking to her when they first set out. Nothing serious, of course—just the quick, light prattle that he knew he did so well. After all, Paris was acutely aware that Janeway might have told this Betazoid things that he would rather not have brought up when he had nowhere to run to. By usurping the onus of initiating conversation, Paris knew he also earned the right to keep the subjects impersonal, amusing, and trivial, and he did his best to keep them that way for the entirety of the journey. Stadi played along gamely enough. She smiled, she laughed, she answered his coy feints and thrusts with brief, well-aimed ripostes, and Paris allowed her to score just enough points to keep her interested in the wordplay, not interested in him.

"Stadi," he said now, alerted to a shift in her mood by the length of the silence spread between them during his study of the station, "you're changing my mind about Betazoids."

She twitched one eyebrow upward, and dipped a self-satisfied nod. "Good."

Paris pulled his feet back to the floor to sit upright. "It wasn't a compliment," he assured her. "Until today, I always considered your people to be warm and sensual. . . ."

This time, the little glimmer of condescending

humor he'd been nurturing in her the whole trip flickered into life again.

"I can be warm and sensual."

"Just not to me."

She turned the full force of her playful annoyance on him. "Do you always fly at women at warp speed, Mr. Paris?"

Paris smiled, giving both of them a point with his reply. "Only when they're in visual range."

It killed the conversation again, but at a point more to Paris's liking. Sitting back in his seat, he felt the impulse thrusters take their velocity down to half, and watched Stadi gently shift the shuttle's approach without pointing out the half-dozen ways she could have done things faster, better, more smoothly. *I'm an observer, after all.* The ultimate in look-but-don't-touch technology.

"That's our ship," Stadi said abruptly. The tight excitement in her voice was distinct, contagious, drawing Paris's attention where she pointed even though he hadn't meant to look. "That's *Voyager.*"

At first, he had trouble locating the ship amid the clutter of alien and Federation vessels daisy-chained around the points of the station's docking pylons. Then his wandering eye caught on the Starfleet emblem that graced the hull of a small, sleek ship that hung poised with her nose kissing the uppermost docking bay. Almost at once, he knew this must be what Starfleet meant to send after the Maquis. Janeway had told him so little about the ship, he didn't really know what to expect, but all he could think now was that this beauty was different from any other starship he'd seen. A slim predator, as swift and tireless as a cheetah.

"Intrepid-class," Stadi volunteered as she glided them closer. "Sustainable cruise velocity of warp factor nine point nine-seven-five. Fifteen decks, crew complement of one hundred forty-one, bioneural circuitry—"

Paris glanced a question at her. "Bioneural?"

The Betazoid nodded, almost absently. "Some of the traditional circuitry has been replaced with gel packs that contain synthetic neural cells. They organize information more efficiently, speed up response time." The smile she flashed him was almost wicked with delight. "Want to take a closer look?"

Paris was certain he would have said yes, but Stadi didn't wait for his answer. Delicate fingers dancing across her helm, she swept them into a smooth arc, lifting them over the top of the station and into an intimate flyby across *Voyager*'s fine-tooled bow, along her flanks, beneath the flash of her belly. Paris drank in every promising line of that magnificent ship with a jealousy that made him both angry and afraid. The low-slung warp nacelles on their short, sturdy pylons hinted at a power that no ship before her had ever possessed, and the smooth blending of her primary and secondary hulls looked almost aerodynamic compared with the blissfully angelic craft who made up her direct ancestors. Paris wanted to fly her—wanted to serve on her—wanted to deserve her in a way he'd sacrificed forever when he drummed himself out of Starfleet on Caldik Prime. If someone had told him then that a few hours of stupid fear would eat all the years of his life worth living, he would have laughed and offered them another beer.

And now . . .

Now, he rode in silence behind a darkened panel, lusting after an existence no longer within his reach, an eternal observer in the whirlpool of his life as it dragged him ever downward, into nothing.

It was like being locked out of the circus. Everybody else hurried off into their bright and busy futures, while Paris got left behind like their empty houses, not even close enough to see the parade.

The inside of DS9 didn't match the promise of her strangely alluring exterior. It looked unfinished, somehow—bare, arching struts visible against every unpainted ceiling and bulkhead, conduits thrumming beneath walkways made of mesh. Even the two civilian security types waiting with stiff-necked patience just beyond the docking bay's hatch looked colorless and undefined. But they were security all the same—Paris had gotten pretty good at recognizing the type while putting in his hours down in Auckland. He was suddenly glad that Stadi had stayed behind to batten things down after docking.

"Mr. Thomas Paris?" The slimmer of the two officers glanced pointedly at the data padd in his hand, making it clear he was identifying Paris, not asking him. "Assigned to the scout ship *Voyager?*"

Paris tightened his grip on the duffel slung over his shoulder, but didn't move forward to meet the approaching pair. "Yeah, that's me."

The skinny spokesman didn't seem impressed by Paris's heartbreaker smile. "My name is Odo. I'm chief of security here on *Deep Space Nine.*" He had a good face for the job—expressionless and inhuman, the skin stretched tight and shiny across nonexistent features, as though some surgeon hadn't been bothered to finish putting things right after a really bad burn. Paris could almost feel sorry for the guy if his presence here hadn't made Paris so angry.

"Can I do something for you, Officer Odo?" Paris didn't mean for the question to sound that sarcastic, but things always seemed to come out of him that way.

Odo tipped his head in a gesture queerly reminiscent of a raised eyebrow. "I just wanted to verify your arrival on the station, Mr. Paris," he said evenly. "And to tell you that if you have any trouble while you're here, you can be sure either myself or my staff will be nearby."

Damn Janeway. Was it really reasonable for her to trust him so little—to expect so much grief—that she thought it necessary to warn local security?

And him only scheduled to be onstation less than two hours. It was all Paris could do to keep the grin stretched against his teeth. "Gee, thanks, Officer Odo. I'm sure everybody here feels a whole lot better with you on the job."

"Hey, mister—!"

Odo raised a single long-fingered hand, and the young security type behind him fell silent, an offended frown rewrinkling his already ridged nose.

"You might want to do something about that attitude of yours, Mr. Paris," Odo commented dryly. "From what I've seen of Starfleet, they don't have much use for sarcasm from their junior officers." A chime sounded from his padd, and Odo spared it only a flick of interest before acknowledging it with a nod. "Now, if you don't mind, there are some more of your shipmates arriving at Docking Ring Two that I'd like to go down and greet." Odo favored Paris with something caught between a disdainful sniff and a scowl. "Welcome to the station."

Some more of your shipmates . . . Paris watched Odo stride purposefully away down the corridor, the young security man at his back spearing Paris with more than one disgusted look before they disappeared around the bend. They'd been greeting everyone, Paris realized suddenly, one at a time as they came in. A courtesy. A true act of professional respect, from members of the civilian constabulary to their Starfleet benefactors. And Paris had pretty much spit on their boots.

It had been a long time since he'd felt quite this humiliated.

My problem, Paris thought as he started his slow, solitary way down a corridor leading away from Odo's retreat, *is that I don't know when to keep my mouth shut.* Well, maybe that wasn't his primary problem, but it certainly exacerbated all the others. He could still hear his father's calm, cultured voice saying, "I'm ashamed of myself, Tom. Ashamed that I've somehow managed to raise a son with so little sense of morality or basic judgment."

Yeah, Dad, I'm ashamed of you, too.

It wasn't hard to wander his way down to the station's main thoroughfare. Paris just let his feet guide him, confident they'd end up outside the nearest bar. He eventually found himself strolling a crowded, gaudy, almost embarrassingly mall-like promenade crammed full of shops, kiosks, and milling patrons. For one disjointed moment, Paris wasn't sure if he was on a Starfleet station or some low-tech planetoid's barter bazaar. At least he could read a good portion of these signs.

The tavern stood out from the rest of the establishments. A lot of the right kind of lights and ambience, none of the really expensive trappings that seemed to come with the low-threat places that liked to play at being bars without actually attracting that kind of clientele. No, this was the real thing. Paris recognized the sounds of pain muttering from a set of Dabo tables, the sturdy-but-just-one-credit-too-nice-to-be-tacky booths and barstools, and that particular blending of synthehol and sweat that meant lots of business, lots of bodies, lots of booze. Someone had told him once that the distinctive blue-gray lighting affected by most human drinking joints was a holdover from when bars on Earth had been filled to bursting with the smoke of burning paper cylinders, all stuffed with various species of nicotine-producing plants. People supposedly drew this smoke into their lungs and purposefully held it there before exhaling. Paris found the idea of this not only unbelievable, but kind of disgusting. Still, he thought of it now as he passed through the tavern's front entrance and was brushed in the face by a cloud of something sooty and stinging that smelled like mint. Rubbing his nose to keep from sneezing, he walked beyond the two grinning goons who passed the burning glass between them, and found a seat at the farthest end of the bar.

". . . and if I may say so, it's been my special pleasure to see many new officers like yourself come through these portals." The bartender—a toady little Ferengi with a vest too flashy and clashing to be worn by anyone but the owner—leaned on his elbows across the polished counter to expose sharklike teeth at a Starfleet ensign with the guileless Asian face of a young Buddha. "I'm sure your parents must be very proud, my boy. You know, on an occasion like this—"

The ensign smiled politely and shook his head. "I'm really not interested."

Paris winced down at the bar top. You should never say "interested" in front of a Ferengi.

"Interested?" the barkeep echoed, his beady blue eyes the very picture of mercantile innocence.

The ensign smiled again. "You were about to try to sell me something. Right?"

Strike two, Paris thought. "Interested" *and* "sell" within the same five minutes. This kid was doomed.

And the barkeep was good. He pushed away from the bar, up to his full diminutive stature, so he could peer at the ensign as though from the height of great moral superiority. "I was merely going to suggest your parents might appreciate a memento of your first mission—"

"—and you happen to have several to choose from."

The Ferengi shrugged as though this were only a minor consideration. "I do carry a select line of unique artifacts and gemstones indigenous to this region. . . ."

Paris ordered a Romulan ale from a waiter too stupid to keep out of his line of vision, then leaned back on his stool to keep the barkeep and the soon-to-be-penniless ensign in his sight. In that brief moment of inattention, a sizable case of sparkling gemstones had materialized on the counter. Paris couldn't help being a little disappointed—he'd been hoping to glimpse how a Ferengi swindler could produce such a large display box from up his sleeve with so little notice.

"Why, quite recently," the barkeep was continuing as he tipped and tilted the case to reveal every stone to its best advantage, "I acquired these Lobi crystals from a very strange creature called a Morn—"

Even as one of the lumpy patrons at the other end of the bar glanced up in apparent recognition, the ensign waved the Ferengi off with a confident and knowing grin. "We were warned about Ferengi at the Academy," he explained—quite civilly.

Paris almost heard the clank of latinum pouring into the Ferengi's pockets.

Setting the tray down with exaggerated care, the barkeep cocked his head at the ensign in earnest disbelief. " 'Warned about Ferengi,' were you . . ." He said it as though no one had ever spoken those words in front of him before.

The ensign nodded with cheerful confidence. "That's right."

"Slurs," the Ferengi clarified. "About my people. At the Academy."

The look of sudden panic on the young ensign's face was almost worth the price of the Romulan ale Paris hadn't yet bothered to touch. "What I meant was—"

"Here I am, trying to be a cordial host, knowing how much a young officer's parents would appreciate a token of his love on the eve of a dangerous mission, and what do I get?" The Ferengi sniffed with barely contained anguish. "Scurrilous insults." A padd appeared in the barkeep's hand almost as miraculously as the gems had, and he was tapping out notes on its face before Paris had even finished smiling about the surgical skill of this Ferengi's technique. "Well, somebody is going to hear about this." He angled a positively predatory glare upward. "What was your name, son?"

"My . . . name?"

The Ferengi snorted at him. "You have one, I presume?"

"Kim," the ensign blurted, eyes wide. "Harry Kim."

"And who was it at the Academy who warned you about—"

"You know," Kim interrupted, his hands a flurry of nervous excitement as he reached across to pluck at the Ferengi's sleeve, "I think a memento for my parents would be a great idea!"

"Oh, no no no." The barkeep pulled himself away as though too hurt to let himself be so easily assuaged.

"Really!" Kim picked up the case and made an obvious effort to study the gaudy contents. "One of these would look great as a pendant for my mother."

"Or cuff links for your father."

"Cuff links," Kim echoed enthusiastically. "Great idea."

"They're not for sale!" The Ferengi jerked the entire display out of the young man's hands with a vehemence that startled Paris and actually made Kim hop back a step. "Now," the barkeep sniffed, bending back to his data padd, "inform your commanding officer that the Federation Council can expect an official query from—"

Kim planted both hands on the tray before the Ferengi could lift it out of sight. "How much for the entire tray?"

"Cash or credit?"

This was too much. As much as he fancied himself a hardened, cynical product of the Federation penal system, even Paris couldn't sit by and watch one of the galaxy's most insidious predators pluck apart a juvenile member of his own species. No matter how much that member so richly deserved it. Abandoning his ale (which was shamefully watered down anyway), Paris moved two stools closer to the barter to comment loudly, "Dazzling, aren't they?"

The Ferengi shot him a look that could have melted a warp core.

"As bright as Koladan diamonds," Paris went on, seating himself directly at the kid's elbow.

The Ferengi almost snarled. "Brighter."

"Hard to believe you can find them on any planet in this system."

The Ferengi slapped his hand away from the case

when Paris would have picked up one of the colored gemstones for study. "That's an exaggeration."

Pretending not to hear him, Paris remarked casually to Kim, "There's a shop at the Volnar Colony that sells a dozen assorted shapes for one Cardassian lek." He tossed the Ferengi a look of calculated innocence. "How much you selling these for?"

"We were just about to negotiate the price. . . ."

Blinking as if recovering from a sharp blow to the head, Kim glanced at Paris, then at the Ferengi, then down at the display case still in front of him. Paris knew just how the kid must feel—Paris has once been stupid enough to try and barter with Ferengi, too. He still had the scars. Shoving the case back across the bar toward its owner, Kim was turned and headed for the door before Paris had even flicked an overpayment for his ale onto the bartop. What the hell—the show had been worth it, even if the liquor hadn't.

Paris found Kim fidgeting just outside the entrance, obviously waiting for him. Kim looked impossibly younger even than he had inside, his cheeks flushed with redness, mortification plain on his face. Paris remembered at least a little of what it had been like to think you were ready for anything, just to have everything around you prove you were wrong.

"Thanks," Kim said simply, glancing away.

Paris clapped him on the shoulder, wishing no one ever had to be this young. "Didn't they warn you about Ferengi at the Academy?" he asked.

Kim looked for a moment like he might try an answer, then gave up and only laughed. Paris was surprised at how much he appreciated that sound.

CHAPTER

3

IT COULD HAVE BEEN WORSE, HARRY KIM TOLD HIM-self. He could have actually been proud as well as stupid, and insisted on taking care of the Ferengi himself instead of backing off when his obviously more worldly-wise shipmate stepped in. But pride —unlike stupidity—had never been one of Kim's big problems. While he figured he ought to be glad for that right now, all he felt was embarrassed, and naive, and young.

Kim glanced aside at the tall, quiet man who'd come to his rescue. *I'll never be that cool,* he thought wistfully. *Or that tall.* There was something desperately unfair about always being the young, adorable one who sparked the protective instincts of strangers all the way on the other end of a bar.

He bet no woman had ever kissed Tom Paris on the cheek and sighed, "You're so sweet!"

The walk to *Voyager*'s berth was more crowded and noisy than long. Kim had arrived on DS9 yesterday—plenty of time to spend too much money at most of the shops, get sick at a Klingon restaurant, attend an extremely strange Tellarite production of *The Cherry Orchard* (in his opinion, they'd beaten the play up pretty badly), and talk himself into a game of racquetball with a friendly medical lieutenant. Even so, he hadn't quite recovered from the breathless excitement that swept him when he returned to the ship after each bold excursion, thinking in amazement, *This is now my home.*

He realized he'd stumbled to a stop in the ship's open hatchway when Paris bumped into him from behind. Keeping his face averted to hide another blush, Kim hurried into the open corridor and waved his companion to follow.

Paris stepped through the portal as though no special emotions moved him, his duffel still balanced on one shoulder. Kim watched the older man glance left and right with the same politeness with which a high-school friend would peruse a classmate's home, and realized that the thrill of hearing his own footsteps on the deck was not the universal phenomenon he'd convinced himself it was. It was just him, Harry Kim, being silly about the romance of what was really just another job.

"This must feel pretty routine to you by now," he

said aloud, trying for a tone of mature nonchalance, "coming on board a new ship. . . ."

A strange, crooked grin accompanied Paris's short laugh, and the older man shook his head. "Not exactly."

That odd response reassured Kim somehow. "I guess your first posting is the one you never forget. When I came aboard this morning, I couldn't help it . . . I got goose bumps. . . ."

"Yeah." The peculiar distance left Paris's eyes, and he smiled at Kim with the warmth of memories shared by only a few of Starfleet's best. "I remember feeling like that."

And it suddenly didn't seem so dumb that Kim felt that way now. "Have you checked in yet?" When Paris only shook his head, Kim smiled and waved him to follow. "Come on—I'll take you to sickbay."

"Sickbay?" Paris stopped long enough to swing his duffel across to the other shoulder, then hurried after Kim to keep up. "Why don't we check in up on the bridge?"

"Uh, I'm not sure, exactly." In fact, it hadn't even occurred to him to ask. "I haven't been up to the bridge yet," he admitted with a little discomfort. "But Dr. Fitzgerald's always down in sickbay, it seems, and he's the most senior officer next to the captain and First Officer Cavit."

Paris dipped a wry nod of acceptance. "Then sickbay it is." He gestured forward with one hand. "Lay on, Macduff."

They made most of the trip in silence. Kim meant to instigate conversation at least two or three times during the twenty-minute walk, he really did. But, somehow, his Academy-trained mind couldn't manage to compose any sufficiently intelligent opener between the station dock and the sickbay, so they passed the time in what Kim felt was an intolerable silence while Paris whistled to himself and peeked inside every open cabin they passed. Even once they reached the sickbay entrance, all Kim could think to do was indicate the double doors and announce, "Well . . . here it is," as though stating the obvious had been his major course of study since joining Starfleet.

At least Paris only answered with a grin and a nod before stepping inside.

The infirmary was tiny although well equipped, hardly busy yet with most of the crew only just getting settled in their quarters and the station's docking clamps still firmly engaged. Dr. Fitzgerald was busying himself with an array of incomprehensible computer panels against one wall, just as he had been since the first time Kim walked in here, several hours ago. Something about the doctor's blunt, florid features had struck Kim as unfriendly even then; watching him gesture impatiently at his calm Vulcan assistant now didn't do anything to improve the young ensign's initial impression.

"Run a level-three diagnostic," Fitzgerald was saying irritably, as though the Vulcan were the stupidest creature he'd ever had to endure. "Just to be sure—" He turned to call something after her as she moved away, and his eyes caught on Kim and Paris in the doorway, as though he was more than just a little scandalized by their interruption. "Can I help you?"

Kim felt familiar embarrassment push itself surfaceward, and was angry for letting the doctor trigger that when he hadn't done anything wrong.

"Tom Paris, reporting on board." Paris announced himself with an easy confidence Kim envied, even when it earned the older man a glare of pure disapproval from the ill-tempered physician.

"Oh, yes . . . the . . ." What could only be disgust twisted the doctor's full mouth. ". . . 'observer' . . ."

Paris nodded, grin in place but eyes wary. "That's me." He waited a moment, letting the silence between them stretch until Kim felt almost compelled to break it. Then, just before the ensign would have interfered, Paris remarked jauntily to Fitzgerald, "As a matter of fact, I seem to be observing some kind of problem right now . . . Doctor."

Fitzgerald flashed a grin that never even showed his teeth, much less any true emotion. "I was a surgeon at the hospital on Caldik Prime the same time you were stationed there." Something closer to delight glittered in the doctor's eyes at whatever happened to Paris's expression. But when Kim glanced quickly up at his companion, he could find nothing but Paris's smile. "We never actually met," the doctor went on.

Paris nodded as though that explained everything, but said nothing.

Fitzgerald turned away from him to toy with a data chip on an exam table nearby. "Your medical records arrived from your last . . . 'posting,' Mr. Paris." He looked at Paris over the chip. "I think everything's in order. The captain asked if you're on board. You should check in with her."

"I haven't paid my respects to the captain yet, either." Kim tugged gingerly at Paris's elbow, silently urging him to take the out they'd been given before the air got too thick with tension to breathe.

"Well, Mr. Kim," Fitzgerald told him, apparently thinking the same thing, "that would be a good thing for the new operations officer to do."

Yeah, and the hell with you, too, Kim caught himself thinking. He ducked into the corridor in an agony of dismay, wondering insanely what his mother would say to hear him entertaining such impolite thoughts about his superiors. Waiting for the door to hush shut behind them, he looked up at Paris and asked, "What was *that* all about?"

To his surprise, Paris only sighed and clapped him on the back. "It's a long story, Harry, and I'm tired of telling it." He tried out a grin too tired to make it to his eyes. "I'm sure someone around here will tell you before long."

The only problem was, Kim wasn't entirely sure it would be something he wanted to hear.

CHAPTER
4

TOO MUCH TO DO. FAR, FAR TOO MUCH TO DO, AND NOT
even an hour now until launch. Janeway blinked
herself back from another mental tally of the
subspace queues she still had to sort through, and
found herself staring at two mugs of coffee in the
tray of the ready-room replicator with no memory
of having ordered either one. It was Mark's voice
over the monitor behind her, she realized with a
pang of bittersweet amusement. When he was over
for one of her all-night preparatory binges, they
always took turns fetching coffee for each other.
She called up a mug for him by habit. Only this
time, she couldn't pass it over to him, or receive his
kiss in return.

Picking up one of the warm ceramic cups, she

did her best to tuck a few stray data padds under her arm so she wouldn't have to make two trips. Even so, she had to let the padds fall into a shamefully disorganized pile on the table she'd commandeered as she settled her coffee safely beyond the reach of her elbows.

"The doctor called," Mark told her, as though she'd never walked thoughtlessly out of his sight in the middle of his previous sentence. He was used to this sort of chaos just before a mission, Janeway knew.

She took a sip of coffee and picked up the first in a deep pile of reports. "And . . . ?"

"And," he announced smugly, "I was right."

Janeway had to swallow fast to keep from burning her tongue. "She's pregnant?!"

The smile on his face was infuriating enough to have earned him a pinched cheek if he'd been in range. "The puppies are due in seven weeks."

Seven weeks? It seemed like she should have realized what was going on by nearly halfway through a dog's pregnancy. Janeway clapped a hand to her head, barely able to push ship thoughts aside long enough to consider what to do. "Mark," she cried at last, "you've got to take her home with you!"

"With me? I just got the rugs cleaned!"

"She's *with child,*" Janeway objected. It was all she could do to keep from laughing at his far-too-dubious scowl. "I can't leave her in a kennel while I'm—"

"Is this another love-me-love-my-dog demand?" Mark interrupted sweetly.

Janeway smiled at him. "Yes."

He sighed and rolled his eyes in his best imitation of heroic martyrdom. "How could I ever refuse you?"

"Thanks, honey." She meant it for so many things other than Bear, but felt sure Mark already knew that.

"When do you leave?"

The question only reminded her of the landslide of work still crowding the ready-room table, and she glanced down at it with throb of sudden fatigue. "As soon as I approve these system status reports." She picked up one and made herself scan it as she spoke.

"All right," Mark told her. "I won't bother you anymore."

"Hey . . ." Lifting her eyes from the data padd, Janeway reached out to trace the image of his face on her monitor, frustrated by the light-years of distance. "You never bother me," she told him gently. "Except the way I love to be bothered. Understand?"

He reached out for her in turn, the channel stopping both of them just before contact was made. "Aye, Captain."

"See you in a few weeks." A few very short weeks, judging from the speed with which things had happened so far. It hardly seemed long enough to get everything done. "Oh! And, Mark—go by my house and pick up the doggy bed. She'll be more comfortable."

"I already did," he admitted, teasing her. "An hour ago."

Janeway made an attempt to look put out by his humor, but, as usual, couldn't maintain even false irritation with him. Kissing her fingers, she touched his lips on the screen and smiled. *Just a few weeks.* Returning her silent gesture, he winked a jaunty farewell before breaking the channel to leave her to her work.

A mixed blessing, at best. There was certainly a lot of it, although none of it was very hard. An acknowledgment here, a verification there. Janeway affixed her thumbprint to so many differ-ent reports and manifests by the time she'd reached the bottom of her coffee, she was surprised she hadn't worn the ridges away to nothing. At least the stack in the middle of the table was somewhat neater now, and filled with completed work instead of chores yet waiting. Just that minor triumph always had a tendency to calm her somewhat at the start of a mission.

Standing, Janeway carried her empty mug back to the ready room's sole replicator, and was still contemplating whether or not to actually finish off the second coffee or recycle it when the chime to the outside door sounded. "Come in."

She recognized Paris from their brief conversa-tion in Auckland, and the boy—Harry Kim—from the crew manifest she'd filed away earlier that afternoon. Paris was cleaner and a good deal more respectable with his neatly trimmed hair and Starfleet-issue singlet. Kim looked young enough to be thrown out of every drinking joint in the sector, not to mention terrified. "Gentlemen, welcome aboard *Voyager.*"

Paris nodded once, with a certain wry dignity, and Kim made a valiant attempt to pull even more stiffly to attention. "Thank you, sir," the young ensign said breathlessly.

"Mr. Kim . . ." Janeway thumbed a control on the replicator, watching both mugs fade away into nothing. "At ease before you sprain something."

He made what she assumed was an attempt to relax, but not much about his posture changed.

Janeway folded her arms and turned her back on the replicator, regarding him. "Mr. Kim, despite Starfleet protocol, I don't like being addressed as 'sir.' "

He flushed and nodded stiffly. "I'm sorry . . . ma'am?"

" 'Ma'am' is acceptable in a crunch, but I prefer 'Captain.' " She waited for him to acknowledge with a bob of his head, then stepped away from the machinery to gesture toward a door on the far side of the ready room. "We're getting ready to leave. I'll show you to the bridge." They fell into step behind her, Paris trailing a few steps behind as he hefted an underfilled duffel before following. She wondered what he'd had to bring along in the way of personal effects, or if he'd brought whatever was within reach from his quarters in Auckland, just to keep from looking out of place.

"Did you have any problems getting here, Mr. Paris?" She'd meant the question as small talk—so neither Paris nor Kim would feel the obvious difference in their positions because of her uneven attentions—but she knew Paris must have taken it as something more when he answered her glibly, "None at all—*Captain.*"

Well, at least she could be certain the Rehab Committee had sent her the right felon.

The doors separating the ready room from the bridge whisked open on a low but pervasive hum of working machinery. Janeway's whole body responded to the busy sound, stepping into rhythm with this ship and its purpose as easily as a dancer was swept up into the music that made up half her art. Cavit, down by Stadi at the helm, glanced up from their work with a nod, and Janeway returned it with a hint of a smile. As much as she couldn't explain, she loved this ship already—loved the elegance of her powerful brain, loved the efficiency of her design, couldn't wait for an excuse to let her loose and find out what it was like to chase the heels of warp ten. Stepping down to the main command level, she paused to rest her hand on the command chair, but didn't yet take the seat.

"My first officer, Lieutenant Commander Cavit." She motioned Kim and Paris forward as Cavit turned to offer his hand. "Ensign Kim, Mr. Paris," she introduced them each in turn

Cavit hesitated only slightly before taking Paris's hand, but his smile was stiff and unconvincing. "Welcome aboard."

Janeway made a mental note to speak with Cavit later. She'd given him credit for more decorum than that. From the amused but bitter look on Paris's face, however, Paris hadn't.

She distracted Kim by directing him toward the operations console to one side. "This is your station. Would you like to take over?"

He looked a little startled, but smiled widely. "Yes, ma'am."

Janeway resisted an urge to pat him on the head. "It's not crunch time yet, Mr. Kim." She waved him into his seat. "I'll let you know when."

Hands laced behind her back, Janeway made a slow circuit of the bridge—ostensibly for a last stern look over everyone's shoulder, but in truth because she was still enjoying the heady mixture of freedom and responsibility that always came with each new starship command. The bridge itself was small, the synergy among this new crew already bright and strongly active. They were going to be good together, Janeway thought with delight. It was a good ship, and she'd never been so proud to be its captain.

Like an island of discord in the midst of this tentative harmony, Paris stood with his duffel on his feet, looking silently around at all the stations and careers that his past had locked irrevocably away from him. Janeway couldn't find it in her heart to pity him. Coming to terms with the consequences of your actions was one of the harder lessons of growing up, it was true. And, as with all life's lessons, sometimes otherwise promising people got drowned in the backwash of their big mistakes. It might not have been fair, but it was reality. Not even a father in the admiralty could change that. So if Paris couldn't get used to standing by the wayside while *Voyager*'s crew did what they were made for, these next few weeks were only the beginning of his problems—because, judging from what Janeway had seen of him so far, she didn't expect things to change for Paris any time soon.

Stepping down to the command level again, she caught up Cavit's eyes with her own. *It's time,* she thought. And he nodded, as if understanding without the need for words.

"Lieutenant Stadi—" The first officer's voice rang out across the busy bridge, locking in everyone's attention. "Lay in the course and clear our departure with operations."

Stadi nodded, bending to her console with fingers already dancing across the controls. "Course entered. Ops has cleared us."

"Ready thrusters."

"Thrusters ready," Kim announced, a little too loudly. Janeway smiled at the nervous excitement in his voice.

I know just how you feel.

Seating herself in the captain's chair, she forced

herself to sit calmly relaxed while every neuron inside her jittered with expectation. It wouldn't do for the captain to fidget as they took the ship away from the station. Taking a deep breath in preparation for all the things to come, she lifted her chin and commanded simply, "Engage."

CHAPTER
5

NOT A GOOD START FOR THE DAY, TOM PARIS DECIDED as he paused inside the mess hall to yawn and rub the back of his neck. Less than twenty-four hours on board *Voyager*, and he'd already managed to look like an idiot in front of the entire bridge crew and still find time to get a lousy night's sleep. He'd told himself it was the bed—far too soft and well contoured after his accommodations at the penal colony—and that the silence in his sterile ship's quarters felt too unnatural after the raucous New Zealand nights. But tuning up a track of environmental "music" hadn't done much to derail the loop of frustrated thoughts whirling around in his head, and transferring to his cabin floor hadn't made him any more comfortable than the bed had.

Deprived of even such harmless illusions, Paris finally had to admit that he couldn't sleep because he was nervous, and uncertain, and desperate to impress somebody, *any*body, on this mission.

And now this.

Kim was the first to look up from the little coffee klatch, and the only one with the grace to look embarrassed. Cavit and Fitzgerald didn't even bother to avert their eyes when Paris looked directly at them, as though they had a right to be here talking about him and he wasn't even fit to breathe the same air. Painfully aware that they were probably right, Paris made his way to the bank of food replicators even though he didn't feel very hungry anymore.

"Tomato soup."

The machine whirred to itself for a moment, but no food appeared on its open pad. "There are fourteen varieties of tomato soup available from this replicator," a polite female voice informed him. "With rice. With vegetables. Bolian-style—"

"Plain." He was a purist.

"Specify hot or chilled."

Paris thumped his forehead against the wall and contemplated the likelihood of even the computers on board this ship conspiring against him as a worthless example of the species that created them. "Hot," he said with some vehemence. "Hot, plain tomato soup." It seemed nothing in his life was ever as easy as it ought to be.

By the time the replicator had worked out all the refinements and produced a single bowl of plain tomato soup, Cavit and Fitzgerald were gone and Paris was left with the too-hot bowl in both hands, staring across the room at Kim as the ensign suddenly found himself both fascinated by and utterly disinterested in his food. Paris tried not to be angry with the kid. *Hey,* he told himself, *you knew it couldn't last.* And yet, just as he'd hoped Janeway really meant to give him a second chance on board *Voyager,* he'd also hoped his past would leave him be long enough to choose his own direction for a change. *I guess even warp 9.9 isn't fast enough for that.*

He slipped into the seat across from Kim and ducked forward a little to catch the younger man's eye when Kim wouldn't look up from his food. "There, you see?" Paris said, trotting out his best carefree smile to try and drive away the discomfort between them. "I told you it wouldn't take long."

Kim stared at his tray a moment longer, then seemed to make some powerful decision and lifted his eyes to meet Paris's smile with grim sincerity. "Is it true?"

I don't know "true" anymore, he wanted to say, but heard his mouth answer, "Was the accident my fault? Yes. Pilot error. But it took me a while to admit it." What little bravery he possessed failed him, and he found himself studying the surface of his soup just to have somewhere else to look. It looked more orange than red, and smelled vaguely like ginger. "Fourteen varieties, and they can't even get plain tomato soup right. . . ."

"They said you falsified reports. . . ."

Paris nudged his not-quite-soup with a spoon. "That's right."

Kim set his own utensils down to lean across the table. *"Why?"* As if the idea would never even occur to him—as if he couldn't even imagine a situation where doing something so stupid would seem like an acceptable idea.

"What's the difference?" Paris said, feeling stupid now for expecting anyone as squeaky-clean as Kim to understand. "I lied."

"But then you came forward," Kim persisted, "and admitted it was your fault."

Paris looked up at him and shrugged. It was the most honest thing he could think to do, and even so it didn't mean much. "I'll tell you the truth, Harry," he sighed, pushing his soup aside. "All I had to do was keep my mouth shut, and I was home free. But I couldn't. The ghosts of those three dead officers came to me in the middle of the night and taught me the true meaning of Christmas. . . ." Suddenly embarrassed by his own confession, he waved the worst of it away. "So I confessed," he finished, somewhat lamely. "Worst mistake I ever made. But not the last. After they cashiered me out of Starfleet, I went out looking for a fight, and I found the Maquis. . . ." He snorted at the memory. "And on my *first* assignment, I was caught."

Kim played with his own food for a while, his dark eyes thoughtful. "Must have been especially tough for you," he said at last, then added, "Being the son of an admiral."

Without wanting to, Paris pictured his father the way he'd looked toward the end of the hearing, and couldn't help wondering why he seemed to have no memories of his father from any happier times. "Frankly, I think it was tougher on my father than it was on me."

Standing, he picked up his useless soup and carried it back to the replicator to throw it out. Why should soup get more credit for being what it wasn't than he did?

"Look," he told Kim as he slid the bowl into the slot, "I know those guys told you to stay away from me." He looked over his shoulder. "And you know what? You ought to listen to them. I'm not exactly a good-luck charm."

Kim shook his head, a frown settling in between his eyes. "I don't need anyone to choose my friends for me." And he smiled, as though proud of his decision.

Paris laughed to himself and rubbed at his eyes. *It wouldn't hurt to have some help,* he thought. *Especially if your choice in friends doesn't get any better than me.* But before he could make himself say as much out loud, his comm badge chirped and made him jump. He hadn't realized until then how long it had been since he'd lived with that sound.

"Janeway to Paris."

Paris tapped his badge, liking the feel of being part of a network again. "Go ahead."

"Report to the bridge," Janeway told him. "We're approaching the Badlands."

Paris recognized the Badlands the minute he stepped onto the bridge. Not the configuration of the stars and nebulae so much as the ribbons and flashes of plasma anger lashing and flaring against that blackness like so much wildfire. It had given him a chill in the pit of his stomach when he'd first piloted into the mess with Chakotay, no matter how smug the big Indian sounded when he promised that no Maquis ship had been torn apart by the storms—at least not recently. Then, Paris had consoled himself with the knowledge that Starfleet didn't have any ships both small enough and weaponed enough to come after the Maquis while they were inside the Badlands protection. Now, standing on the bridge of the very ship built to terrier them out, he felt foolish for that earlier confidence, and worried that his current feelings of safety were just as poorly founded.

Janeway glanced up from the tactical station at the whoosh of the opening doors, her face the same mask of welded neutrality it had been since Paris first laid eyes on her in Auckland. He had to give her credit for that—it was pretty clear she didn't like him, but at least she didn't feel the need to broadcast her opinion to the rest of the crew. Unlike Cavit, who moved only grudgingly away from the captain's shoulder to give Paris access to the console when Janeway waved him over.

And good morning to you, too, Mr. Cavit, Paris thought at him with what he knew was an annoying cordial grin. The first officer must be setting some kind of personal record today for making a pest of himself on someone else's time.

"The Cardassians gave us the last known heading of the Maquis ship." Janeway gathered Paris's attention by reaching over the security officer's shoulder to tap at one of his tactical displays. Whether she was oblivious of Cavit's silent harassment or simply choosing to ignore it, Paris couldn't tell. "And we have charts of the plasma-storm activity the day it disappeared. With a little help, we might be able to approximate its course."

Following her lead—whatever it was—Paris turned his shoulder to Cavit and bent over the tactical console for a better view of the readout. Plasma discharge blinked and retreated in random blossoms all over the screen, with the glowing, jagged line of the Maquis's course dancing back and forth throughout it. The Cardassians had inserted a black marker at the point where they'd been forced to break pursuit, and a dotted line showing how far their sensors had tracked the Maquis after that. "I'd guess they were trying to get to one of the M-class planetoids in the Terikof Belt."

"That would take them here," Cavit explained to the security officer without having to be asked, leaning just a little uncomfortably beyond Paris to point at one corner of the officer's screen.

The security lieutenant nodded, and the image on his display flickered and rebuilt itself, flickered and regrew again. "The plasma storms would have forced them in this direction."

Janeway nodded. "Adjust our course to match," she told Cavit.

"Aye, Captain."

The first officer seemed perfectly happy to disengage himself from the knot around the tactical panel, trotting almost all the way around the upper deck before stepping down to confer with Stadi at the helm. *Ah, Stadi.* She'd been half-friendly on the trip out. Now, she didn't even spare him a glance as she set about executing the instructions she got from Cavit. Oh, well. Paris bid her farewell with a tiny sigh as he followed Janeway down toward her captain's chair.

"The Cardassians claim they forced the Maquis ship into a plasma storm, where it was destroyed." Janeway settled into her chair with a frown. "But our probes haven't picked up any debris."

"A plasma storm might not leave any debris," Paris pointed out.

Janeway shook her head, glancing up at him. "We'd still be able to pick up a resonance trace from their warp core." Which was true, so Paris didn't offer any further suggestions.

"Captain . . ." Kim turned halfway in his seat, as

though afraid to lift his hands from the controls. "I'm reading a coherent tetryon beam scanning us."

Janeway sat forward again. "Origin, Mr. Kim?"

He swung back toward his instruments. "I'm not sure," he admitted. Then he blinked suddenly, and hesitated for a moment before his hands flashed over his console again. "There's also a displacement wave moving toward us. . . ."

The captain rose to her feet. "Onscreen."

Energy as white and coherent as Paris had ever seen exploded across the viewscreen when Kim brought up the image. Even knowing there must be hundreds of thousands of kilometers between the ship and that seething wave of distortion, Paris had to brace one hand against the back of the command chair to keep from jumping back as Kim increased the magnification.

Janeway moved a few steps closer to the monstrous image, as though she might yet see something the ship's computers couldn't tell them. "Analysis."

"Some kind of polarized magnetic variation," Kim reported.

Cavit leaned over the rail from next to the tactical station. "We might be able to disperse it with a graviton particle field."

Janeway nodded without turning to him. "Do it."

Cavit hurried to wave the security officer away

from the panel as the captain announced, "Red alert," and touched a hand to Stadi's shoulder "Move us away from it, Lieutenant."

"New heading," the pilot confirmed. "Four-one-mark-one-eight-zero."

"Initiating graviton field," Cavit chimed in, and Paris felt the whole ship tremble as the first officer launched the powerful burst on its way.

Unlike the advancing displacement anomaly, there was no visual track to follow as the graviton field swelled out beyond the bow of the ship and met up with the onrushing enemy. Paris thought he glimpsed a quick flutter in the displacement wave's integrity at about the point when he knew it and the field would likely cross paths. But it wasn't a clear or distinctive image, and an instant later he heard Kim announce nervously, "The graviton field had no effect," and knew he must have imagined the breach. His heart started to thunder inside him.

"Full impulse," Janeway commanded.

Stadi obeyed without acknowledgment, the ship humming with power as she brought it about. Paris wished suddenly, emphatically, for a station at which to sit, some way to be useful, to help.

Kim remained glued to his readouts. "The wave will intercept us in twenty seconds . . ."

"Can we go to warp?"

Stadi shook her head, still frantically working her controls. "Not until we clear the plasma field, Captain."

". . . eight seconds . . ."

Clearing the space in two swift strides, Janeway slapped at the intercom on the arm of her command chair. "Brace for impact!"

". . . three . . ."

The captain's voice still echoed in the decks below them as the hand of God seized hold of the ship and flung it into the void.

Stadi swallowed a scream as the very fabric of her reality splintered into a hundred unique cries of desperation and pain. She hunched over the conn, fighting for control of her mind now that control of the ship was impossible. *Personal discipline must come first,* a voice from far in her past told her gently. *After this, all other things will follow.*

But how could one find peace when the empathy that bound a Betazoid so strongly to her crewmates was twisted back against her as a torture? All her early fears about close contact with the mentally powerful but untrained human race crashed over her in a horrifying wave of regret.

"How can you stand it?" she'd asked her aunt. She remembered being small, and reed-flat, not yet having come into the womanhood that would give her full understanding of the control her aunt seemed to wear so effortlessly, like a comfortable robe. "All their thinking, all their feeling, *all* the time!"

Aunt Shenzi had lived with humans for longer than Stadi had even been alive at this time. A government worker of some sort, whose interactions with the human-run Federation kept her locked away on Earth for sometimes years at a time. "It isn't all the time," she told Stadi. "Only when they feel about something very strongly."

From what little Stadi had seen, with humans that was almost always. "But don't they take away your *self?*" Stadi had protested. "Crisa says humans push their emotions all over you, until you can only feel what *they* feel, and none of what you really are." Crisa was seventeen, and had been to a Federation reception the year before where all of the young Starfleet ensigns had asked her to dance.

"Crisa isn't exactly a model of personal shielding," Aunt Shenzi had pointed out with a frown. Which was true—half the time, Crisa dithered and fussed because of some other Betazoid's emotions as much as because of her own. "A little leakage from human emotions is bothersome at times," Stadi's aunt went on, "but hardly the monster Crisa makes it out to be. You'll see."

And now, years and years later, Stadi finally *did* see. She saw an admiral with a great mane of white hair scowling down at her with fatherly disapproval—a woman with warm, smiling eyes too wise and patient for her years—a man and a dog tumbling together in the overlong grass, with a lover's amused voice admonishing them to be *careful,* or they'd get dirty. But it was other people's memories, other people's lives, swimming to surround her in that eternal nowhere moment that marked their disappearance from the Badlands and their arrival at—she didn't know. Death? Was this the fabled instant when one's life flashed before your eyes? *And here I am with someone else's life,* Stadi thought with startling clarity. Just as Crisa had warned. Just as Stadi had feared for herself all those years before.

Not just their lives. Aunt Shenzi's voice tickled her thoughts as though she were standing right by Stadi's ear, petting back her hair. *Their lives, and your life, and all of you blessed because of it.* Aunt Shenzi had died seven years ago, when she and the human woman she'd lived with for so long were on a passenger ship destroyed by the Borg. *Come tell me all about it, dear.*

It would be like going home, Stadi thought with a shudder of relief. She could leave all the noise of human panic behind, and embrace an emotional quiet she hadn't known since leaving Betazed for the Academy. She'd miss the humans' lively inner chatter, but she would welcome Aunt Shenzi's promised peace even more.

All right, Aunt Shenzi, I'm coming. She felt the ship burst suddenly out of its darkness, into a light so bright and burning she could feel it blasting through her face, her hands, her chest. Surely this was *Voyager*'s death throes, and what she felt jolting beneath her was the explosion that threw it to pieces. The searing light seemed to throw her upward, out of herself, away from all the noise and terror, away from all the fear and pain. Smiling, Stadi reached out to embrace her Aunt Shenzi, and they moved away together, into silence.

The viewscreen was filled with tracers of light. Like ribbons of the plasma they were trying so hard to avoid, First Officer Cavit thought. Or the ion trail of a dying ship, reaching out to entangle them and drag *Voyager* and everyone aboard her down its mouth to a nowhere place that even the Maquis couldn't escape. Stars ceased to exist, time almost shattered to a standstill, even the powerful forward momentum of a starship in warp drive seemed to thin out into nothingness until it faded from Cavit's senses like the falling Doppler shift of a retreating scream. They were suspended in amber, pinned in place against the motionless velvet of a space-time anomaly.

Then, with a crash, reality spun into wild motion again, and that transcendent moment of timelessness was lost.

Cavit felt a wash of killing heat as the helm panel at the front of the bridge exploded with a booming roar. Quite unconscious of his movements, he turned toward the sound. A million fears fought for prominence in his head—fear of an oxygen-stealing fire, fear of a gas leak, or, worst of all, a total hull breach—but he never had the chance to find out which of those many deaths was the true one. A hard wall of violently compressed air swatted him over the bridge railing, onto the upper deck, and all the breath rushed out of him as though he'd been punched by a giant's invisible hand. He hit the floor on his shoulder, felt the socket push against itself with the force. Whatever had racked the ship before still held her, flinging her the way a dog would fling a helpless rabbit, and Cavit struggled to stop himself when the rough pitching rolled him uncontrolled beneath the feet of the officer at the engineering console. They both tumbled against the panel. Cavit smelled blood— whether on himself or on the engineer, he couldn't tell—just as he slammed the base of the machinery with the engineer's weight pinning him to the floor.

The very first ship Cavit had ever served on board was a Starfleet colony-relief transport, some ten or fifteen years ago. He'd been a young ensign then, not even out of the Academy, really. They'd sent half his class out on short-term noncombat hauls as part of some new curricular plan, giving them the chance to experience the reality of what they all thought they wanted to train to do. A chance to get their feet wet, in a manner of speaking.

Cavit had thought it the most exciting assignment in the world at the time. The *U.S.S. Kingston* had ferried scientists and medicines, animals and supplies, to every growing colony between Miracle and Cimota VI. It had seemed like there could be nothing so romantic, nothing more important than bestowing on mankind's most remote bastions the very elements of life they needed for their everyday survival. He had felt like a young god, bringing blessings from the stars to every planet on their itinerary. The *Kingston*'s CPO, Russ Tepper, had laughed to hear Cavit admit to his feelings, but even that had never changed the young man's private views.

Then, while the *Kingston* was shipping stock gametes from the Vulcan genetic yards to Rukbat III, Orion pirates swept down on them and carved their hull apart.

The Orions had thought the *Kingston* was carrying latinum to a processing plant in the Ganges Sector, where it would be smelted and put to use in all its various valuable forms. The pirates were on board and reaving through whatever crew stood up to fight them before they discovered their mistake. By then it was too late for the Orions to back away as though nothing at all had happened. If they left without murdering every member of the *Kingston*'s crew, then there would be witnesses who had seen the Orions, seen their ship, identified its engine patterns so that the Federation authorities could hunt down the Orions to a man and bring them before the fair but efficient Federation court of law. Worse yet, they might be turned over to their own government, which had some particularly unpleasant ways of dealing with privateers who were stupid enough to be caught by the Federation. The Orions had no choice, as far as their limited views of morality took them—they had to clear the decks and make it look like some other brand of raiders did the dirty work before running with their tails between their legs for the hiding places in their own sector of space. If this crew was composed of primarily unarmed workers and untried ensigns, well, it was merely one of the casualties of doing "business" with the Orions.

Cavit had been so young then, so eager to please his superiors, to do what he'd been told. When Russ Tepper grabbed him and the other frightened cadets, Cavit had been more than willing to follow the CPO to any part of the ship he said—to do anything Tepper or another officer told him to. Because doing what your COs said was right. If all else failed, you could just follow orders, and everything would be fine.

Tepper had crammed sixteen young men and women into the far aft cargo bays, inside and between as many different gamete-transport pods as he could turn off and move. By the time the Orions reached those smallest bays, they'd already discovered their error, and weren't looking to spend any more time among this essentially worthless payload. They'd left the bays—and the sixteen people inside them—without even turning off the lights. Cavit had huddled in silence, just as Tepper commanded, until the *Enterprise* arrived two days later to clean up what was left of the terrible slaughter.

He'd done the right thing, a dozen commodores and admirals had told him in the years to follow.

All those young people had been so smart, so brave, so loyal, to hide themselves as ordered while their captain and crew all died. Because of them, the tragedy was exposed for what it really was, and the Orions who had perpetrated the horrible crime had been hunted down and punished as laid out by Federation law. Cavit had never attended the trials. All he knew was that—despite the commendations, despite all the glowing words Starfleet's finest might heap upon him—in his heart he still felt like a traitor for having done nothing while his first ship was murdered. He went to sleep every night praying for forgiveness, and promising himself that if any ship on which he served was ever threatened again, he would die rather than forsake her crew.

I won't let it happen again!

Pushing the lifeless engineer off him, Cavit dragged himself out from under the console and onto his knees. He didn't know if emergency lighting had failed to come immediately, or if that first great explosion had blinded him, but he stumbled upright without being able to see, and felt for the railing with both hands. *It won't happen again,* he promised himself. *My ship, my captain, my crew— I'll die before I disown them!*

When he heard the creak and crack of collapsing metal above him, some dispassionate part of Cavit knew it was the ceiling giving way. He lifted his head, sightless eyes searching the darkness above him, but couldn't tell which way to step to save himself. He was still gripping the handrail, hating himself for his weakness, when the crush of falling debris drove him back down to the deck for the final time.

"Report!"

Paris jerked back into awareness at the sound of Janeway's barked command. He blinked, reaching out to feel something familiar, something useful he could tell her, and realized with a jolt that he was facedown on the main deck with smoke and fire licking at him from all sides. He struggled to his knees, but couldn't seem to remember which way he should turn.

"Hull breach, Deck Fourteen!" Kim had already made it back to his panel, scanning through screen after screen of information despite a fist-sized bruise across his cheekbone and a long streak of burn up one arm. "Comm lines to engineering are down—trying to reestablish . . ."

Paris stumbled toward where Stadi sprawled, unmoving, beside the shattered helm console. Behind him, he heard Janeway kicking aside debris from the collapsed ceiling, and realized belatedly that the smear of black-and-red he could glimpse inside that tangled wreckage was someone's broken body.

"Repair crews!" Janeway shouted to raise her voice above both the sirens and the clanging of her fight with the bridge wreckage. "Seal off hull breach on Deck Fourteen—"

"Casualty reports coming in," a new voice called from the tactical console. "Sickbay is not responding."

Stadi rolled limply when Paris pulled on her shoulder. This was a mistake, he realized the moment she sagged onto her back and exposed her burned, unseeing eyes. He shouldn't have expected anyone to survive an explosion the size of what destroyed the pilot's console, shouldn't feel this throb of frustrated grief and anger over something he hadn't caused and couldn't control.

"Bridge to sickbay." The captain stood immediately behind him now, apparently having given up her rescue efforts on whoever had been crushed in the ceiling collapse. "Doctor, can you hear me?"

Cavit. The name came to Paris in its own little explosion of understanding. He hadn't heard Cavit since the displacement wave caught them, and Janeway hadn't asked where her first officer was. Which meant she already knew. Janeway moved toward where Stadi lay on the bridge floor.

Taking the captain's composure as his example, Paris stood slowly and turned with what he hoped was a brave expression. "She's dead." If his voice was less than steady, he only hoped the captain would understand.

"Captain . . . ?" Kim interjected. An oddly welcome distraction, if only because Paris wasn't sure how long he could hold up his facade of strength beneath the understanding sympathy in Janeway's eyes. "Captain, something's out there!"

She turned to face him, recrossing the bridge to lean against the railing below him. "I need a better description than that, Mr. Kim."

"I don't know." But he blurted it, and Paris could see the embarrassed color rise into Kim's face as the ensign hurried to compile enough information for a better reply. "I'm reading . . . I'm not sure *what* I'm reading!"

"Can you get the viewscreen operational?"

"I'm trying. . . ."

It sputtered to life with a great roar of static, and Paris whirled to face it as though expecting another attack. Surges and hisses flared across the screen's surface, twining together and apart as the image beyond them fought its way to the foreground. At first, Paris thought it was a city, and that Kim had somehow captured a nearby planet's visual transmission. Then the stars filling the space all around the weird structure gradually faded into view, and Paris realized that what he'd taken for buildings were only the smallest in an eerie collection of struts, arches, and pylons that bristled across the surface of some sort of long, flat orbital structure. Energy pulsed and leapt between the insectoid spires, finally throwing itself out into space where it seared off into distant infinity. Like a lighthouse, Paris thought. Or a radio signal.

Near the belly of the giant array, a tiny speck of matter glittered in the reflections of the great device's waste light. Paris only knew it was the Maquis ship by the trail of text at the bottom of the viewscreen, identifying the stolen vessel's registration.

"Captain . . ." Kim's voice was too quiet, almost numb compared to the chaos around him. "If these sensors are working, we're over seventy thousand light-years from where we were." He looked over at Janeway with an expression too stunned to even be afraid. "We're on the other side of the galaxy!"

CHAPTER
6

THE OTHER SIDE OF THE GALAXY. JANEWAY MOVED CARE-
fully away from Paris and the ruined helm, closing
her hands on the smoke-stained railing so she could
lean on something without showing weakness in
front of her crew.

The other side of the galaxy!

They didn't prepare you to hear things like that
when they trained you at the Academy. Negotia-
tions, combat, the intricacies of shipboard policies
and politics, all the possibilities of starfaring life
that a captain could reasonably look forward to—
these things had filled the days and nights of
Janeway's career, not wild speculation about what
procedures to follow when your Ops officer reports

you've been transported seventy thousand light-years from home.

So she fell back on the basics. "What about the Maquis ship?"

Kim blinked down at his panel as though the smoke still swirling through the bridge were stinging his eyes. "I'm not reading any life signs on the Maquis ship."

"What about that—" Janeway jerked her chin toward the spiny tangle dominating *Voyager*'s main screen. "—that Array?"

"Our sensors can't penetrate it."

She studied the rhythmic flashes throbbing out from the center of the structure, watching them sparkle off into the distance and vanish. "Any idea what those pulses coming from it are, Mr. Kim?"

"Massive bursts of radiant energy . . ." He called up more readings, and Janeway waited as patiently as the current chaos would let her. Down by the viewscreen, Paris had moved Stadi's corpse off to one side and started putting out fires on the helm console. "They seem to be directed toward a nearby G-type star system," Kim reported at last.

"Try hailing the Array," Janeway told him.

The ensign nodded acknowledgment, and Paris looked up from the helm as though waiting for her orders as Janeway made her way around the bridge to push debris away from whatever consoles still functioned. *You're not an officer here,* she thought with some vehemence. *I will not give you even the smallest responsibility under conditions such as this.*

But it wasn't a confrontation she intended to have right now.

The chirp of her comm badge offered an excuse to turn away from Paris's expectant face without specifically dismissing him. She tapped her badge to take the call.

"—Engineering to bridge—" The comm channel spit and shattered with static, but even that couldn't drown the barely controlled panic in Junior Engineer Carey's voice. "We have severe damage—the chief's dead . . . possibility of a warp-core breach . . ."

"Secure all engineering systems," Janeway ordered. "I'm on my way."

Kim looked up as she hurried past him for the turbolift. "No response from the Array."

Not that she'd expected one. That would have been too easy. "Ensign—" She waved Kim away from his position. "Get down to sickbay, see what's going on. Mr. Rollins, the bridge is yours."

She ducked into the lift while the doors were only half open, trying to ignore the sudden clench of her stomach when it occurred to her that the lifts might be dysfunctional and everyone on the bridge relegated to ladders and emergency shafts. But the control panel lit up at a slap from her hand, and the internal system chimed a calm affirmative when she commanded it to go. A last quick glance at the bridge through the closing doors shocked her anew with the damage and death, but what shocked her most of all was the look of open disappointment on

Paris's face as he looked back at her, painfully aware that she had abandoned him there, dutiless, when there was so much on board to be done.

When the ship first trembled as though in response to some great external blow, Dr. Fitzgerald wouldn't let the nurse, T'Prena, call up to the bridge to find out what was going on. As support staff to the great starship, he didn't feel it was their place to be either bothering the command crew during times of crisis, or trying to tell the command crew what they should be doing. "Captains know what's best for their ships," he was fond of saying. "We know what's best for their crew." And, sometimes, what was best was keeping everyone occupied with their assigned duties when there was nothing more useful they could be doing.

Now, Fitzgerald rather wished he had some idea what was happening.

He'd been trying to keep T'Prena busy by using her Vulcan memory instead of a note padd as he ran calibrating samples through the cellular diagnostic sequencer. Distracting a Vulcan, after all, was hardly an easy task—judging whether or not you were successful was a whole other matter entirely. Vulcans didn't fidget or prattle nervously when they were unhappy; they acted the same as they always did. They denied, even, that they could feel unhappy. But a long residency at the Vulcan Science Academy had taught Fitzgerald a lot more than how to gauge a *pon farr* hormonal surge. He'd learned, as well, that Vulcans in many ways felt just as much as humans did; they simply chose not to let those emotions rule their actions and lives. Even when they engaged in behavior for what might otherwise be considered emotional reasons, they made sure they had a logical rationale for doing so. Whether or not that made them emotionless or simply uptight, Fitzgerald had never been able to decide. All the same, he'd realized that once he learned how to recognize the vanishingly subtle clues to Vulcan feelings, he'd begun to appreciate the advantage this gave him as a doctor—the advantage of knowing, just like with human patients, what a Vulcan needed mentally perhaps even before the Vulcan herself did. He was very proud of this skill. It wasn't every doctor who could boast that he knew what was best for a Vulcan, and so Fitzgerald made it a point to do so whenever the opportunity presented itself.

But not in front of the Vulcans, of course.

I was only trying to do what was best. It was all he ever did. He took his duties as protector of the crew's health and welfare very seriously, and would never have done anything to cause any of them harm. Even Paris, to whom he'd spoken so rudely only yesterday—all Fitzgerald wanted was to protect any of the young men and women on board *Voyager* from suffering the same fate as those three poor crewmen on Caldik Prime. All it would take was a boy as trusting and impression-able as young Harry Kim believing Paris when the older man said he was responsible enough to take a shuttle, man the weapons, work the engines, and any one of the one hundred fifty innocent lives on this vessel might be forfeit. That possibility was far more horrible to Fitzgerald than any ill feelings Paris might hold toward him. The doctor had even tried to explain that to Ensign Kim. "It's for the best, you know," he had said quietly over their breakfasts in the mess hall. "Men like that never come to any good." He'd only been trying to protect everyone.

So when the ship lurched mindlessly and pitched the sickbay into darkness, the first thought to race through Fitzgerald's mind was that he had to protect T'Prena. His first wife would have called him a chauvinist, would have claimed he didn't think women—even Vulcan women—were capa-ble of taking care of themselves. But if Fitzgerald had ever given a damn about what anybody thought, he'd probably still be married to at least one of his previous spouses. Throwing his arm around T'Prena's shoulders, he pulled her against him and huddled them both tight against the sequencer, where they could use the wall-mounted unit to help guide them down to the floor, rather than be thrown about the room to smash into whatever examining tables and desks happened to be in the way. The doctor was proud of his quick thinking. "I think it would be best if we tried to make our way into the corridor," he'd started to shout across the darkness.

Then the sequencer exploded.

The percussion of escaping flame and displaced air peeled most of the skin away from his skull and ruptured his eardrums with a clap of brilliant pain. He was glad the shock left him too dumbstruck to scream—his first intake of breath would have seared shut his lungs, leaving him helpless and mute for the five to seven minutes it would have taken him to suffocate. Assuming he remained conscious that long. He struck the deck now in such a state of utter, chilling numbness, he knew his neurological systems must be severely damaged, his blood pressure already plunging below seventy. *Of course—third-degree burns.* Judging from the strange mixture of pain and insensibility cocooning his body, he estimated he'd suffered at least a forty-percent evaporation of skin surface in the initial explosion. That was not an encouraging statistic.

God, you're even starting to phrase your diagnoses like a Vulcan!

T'Prena.

Fitzgerald remembered her with the peculiar jolt of a doctor who has somehow, impossibly, blanked out in the middle of a medical emergency. She wasn't just his nurse, now—if she'd been injured by the sequencer explosion, she was his patient and he had forgotten her. If she was dead, if he had killed her . . . ! He'd never killed anyone in his life. Not through accident, not through error, not even through some ill-thought inaction of his own. He dragged himself blindly across the floor as smoke billowed downward from the fire overhead, and the first sentence of the Hippocratic oath rang in echo to the thunder in his chest. *First, do no harm.*

". . . T'Prena . . . ?"

She was a Vulcan—if she could have answered him, she would have. That thought hugged his heart with pain as he searched for her through a gathering darkness that came from more than just the accumulating smoke. "Nurse . . . ? It's Dr. Fitzgerald . . ." He coughed, and the pain of it nearly tore him apart inside.

He found her with his hands, his eyes too stained with smoke to see her anymore. The front of her uniform was blasted open, stiff along the edges where the fabric had melted and burned. He did his best to avoid all the places where his flesh and muscle would be exposed—he must be filthy, he reasoned, his hands impossibly septic after crawling across this blood- and debris-littered floor. When his hands finally closed on the rounded knob of her shoulder, he groped his way down her arm in search of her wrist. It felt small and cool, the pulse jumping erratically beneath his touch no more than the struggles of a dying bird.

This will not be my fault! I will not let a patient die!

". . . Computer . . ." Fitzgerald heard the console stagger sluggishly to life on the other side of the smoke-filled room. ". . . Initiate emergency . . ." T'Prena's pulse continued to flutter beneath his shaking hand. He held it tighter, willing it to strengthen, willing it to stay.

". . . emergency medical . . ."

It fluttered, thickened, faded . . .

Fitzgerald's breath caught painfully in his chest, and T'Prena felt cold almost the instant her heart stopped beating. *No patient,* he told himself. No reason to fight anymore. He was a doctor, and by his hand a living being had died. Lowering his head to the deck beside her, Fitzgerald closed his eyes to let that swelling final darkness take him.

Engineering glowed like the depths of Hell.

Janeway took a deep breath before striding out of the turbolift, trying to take in a thousand images at once. She counted three dead on the floor just inside the main doors, their bodies reduced to little more than blurred outlines beneath a shroud of torn, discolored tarps. She suffered a sudden, uncomfortable worry about what they were going to do with all these bodies. That wasn't something they talked about much at the Academy, either. A small group of engineers were already helping those of the injured who could walk into the corridor, and someone else knelt beside crew members who were so badly wounded that Janeway couldn't bring herself to believe they would actually survive—even if sickbay was only half this damaged. From speakers out of sight in the gas clouds overhead, the computer's dry, uninflected voice droned, "Warning. Warp-core microfracture. Breach imminent . . . Warning. Warp-core . . ."

Janeway pushed between two suited engineers to grab Carey by the shoulder. "What's the warp-core pressure?"

He twisted about at the sound of her voice, his face a study in frustrated dread. "Twenty-one hundred kilopascals and falling."

"Lock down the magnetic constrictors."

"Captain . . ." He followed her deeper into the engine room, waving silent commands to the two engineers with him as he went. "If we lock them down, at these pressure levels, we might not be able to reinitialize the dilithium reaction."

". . . Warning. Warp-core microfracture . . ."

"We haven't got a choice," Janeway told him. *About being here, about surviving this, about any of it.* "We've got to get the reaction rate down before we try to seal it."

Otherwise the rest of it wouldn't matter. And, for Janeway, that just wasn't an option.

Damn her. *Damn* her, anyway! She'd looked him straight in the eye, acknowledged his presence next to Stadi's lifeless form, and then excluded him as though he were the enemy on her bridge. What did she think he would do? How badly did she think he could screw up, compared to all the damage already done?

Is that how you have to measure yourself now, Paris? In relation to how much worse you can make a situation?

And what proof did he really have that Janeway wasn't right?

"I'm reading fires inside." Kim's voice interrupted his brooding, jerking Paris back to the dark, cluttered corridor just outside the sickbay doors and the sickly stench of burning meat from somewhere within. He'd followed Kim out of the bridge for lack of anything more useful to do. At least putting things together down here would amount to something, would help other members of the crew even if Janeway didn't think Paris had what it took. "We'll have to be careful when we open the doors," Kim said.

Assuming they could get them open. Leaving the ensign to stare at his tricorder, Paris banged on the emergency panel to the left of the entrance until it popped open, dropping half its contents with a startling clatter. Kim jumped around with a gasp, and Paris waved him over as he pulled the fire extinguisher loose from its mount. "Take this," he said, trading the extinguisher for Kim's tricorder with a smile he didn't entirely feel. "I'll go in first—I'm expendable."

Kim gave him a startled look, but only nodded mutely and brandished the extinguisher like a phaser as Paris moved up to the door.

Smoke belched over them in a rotten-smelling wave the instant Paris keyed the doors aside. Coughing into his arm, Paris stumbled into the darkness with the tricorder pushed out in front of him in search of life. Bright, fat sparks dripped like molten gold from a panel in the sickbay's far wall, and Kim darted across to smother the fire in chemicals while Paris made his way toward the two bodies tangled around each other at the base of the console. He knew Fitzgerald and the nurse were dead even before the tricorder confirmed his fears.

"They must have been right next to the console when it exploded." He closed the tricorder to silence it.

Overhead fans roared into life, the overhead lights brightening as power rallied from somewhere and began to sluggishly waken damaged consoles. Pulling a sheet from one of the examining tables, Paris draped it hastily across the two bodies. Already the echo of approaching voices sounded in the corridor outside—wounded arriving, no doubt, and many more to come. Paris could imagine few things less heartening than stumbling through the sickbay doors only to find your doctor lying dead.

"Computer!" Kim ran to meet the first arrivals, a burned, battered group in engineering gold. "Initiate emergency medical holographic program!"

A sparkle of what Paris took at first to be a

transporter tingled through the damaged room. Then, waiting impassively by one of the examining tables, a nondescript man in Starfleet blue suddenly appeared at Kim's elbow as the ensign struggled to lift an unconscious engineer onto the bed. Paris shook off his startlement and hurried over to help.

"Please state the nature of the medical emergency." The new arrival peered keenly at the growing flood of patients from the corridor outside.

"Multiple percussive injuries," Kim told him, and the hologram flashed into action as though activated by a switch. In less time than it took Paris to scrub the sting of sweat from his eyes, the pseudo-doctor was on the other side of the sickbay, bent over a leg wound to peel back the burned cloth.

Something like the registering of information flickered through the hologram's eyes, but no expression reached his face. "Status of your doctor?" he asked as his hands moved up the patient.

Paris only shrugged when Kim glanced up at him. How did you explain to a computer program that the entire ship's butt was in a very flimsy sling?

"He's dead," Kim answered at last, and the hologram in turn responded promptly, "Point four cc's of trianoline."

Kim moved a few uncertain steps forward. "Trianoline?"

The doctor lifted his head, fixing Kim with an expression of chill impatience that Paris could only assume had been programmed in—accidentally or otherwise—from whatever real physician had been the template for this AI. The look certainly had the same effect on Paris that smart-assed doctors always did—he felt stupid and more than a little resentful as he volunteered, "We lost our nurse, too."

That answer was apparently enough, although it didn't do much to ease the hologram's peevish expression. In a blink, the doctor was at one of the scattered medical cabinets, selecting a hypo and a canister of spray. "How soon are replacement medical personnel expected?"

"That's going to be a problem. . . ." Kim had to turn almost in a complete circle to follow the hologram's lightning-fast return to the patient's bedside. "We're pretty far away from replacements right now."

The doctor cleaned and sealed the leg wound with a speed and thoroughness Paris suspected as all for the best, as far as recovery was concerned. The pilot couldn't help thinking it was a good thing the engineer was unconscious, though—it didn't look like Doc Holodeck's handling of the leg had taken little things like discomfort or bedside manner into account.

"Tricorder." He was at another bed instantly, one hand thrust out as he probed the livid bruise on a new patient's forehead despite the young woman's hisses of protest.

Not sure what else to do, Paris tossed his

tricorder to Kim and let the ensign press the device into the hologram's grasp. From the way the kid jerked back from the doctor's touch, Paris guessed that hologram hands didn't exactly make up for the feel of real human skin pressed against your own. He made a vow to himself never to get hurt on this mission if he could avoid it.

The doctor glanced at the tricorder, then pushed it back at Kim in brusque rejection. *"Medical* tricorder."

The ensign nodded, flushing in realization, and darted between a half-dozen other waiting patients to retrieve the right device. The hologram took it from him this time with no particular sign of thanks.

"A replacement must be requested as soon as possible. I'm programmed only as a short-term emergency supplement to the medical team."

Paris laughed a little at the thought of how many of them on this ship would have to serve as emergency supplements for each other in the next few days. "Well, we may be stuck with you for a while, Doc."

The hologram glanced up in what Paris almost mistook for insulted surprise. But that was his own projected feelings of inadequacy from being faced with a nonphysical program that had more responsibility than he did. A classical what-was-the-world-coming-to sort of thing.

The doctor looked away again to finish applying a

light analgesic spray to the darkening bruise. "There's no need for concern," he remarked to Paris while closing up the tricorder. "I'm capable of treating any injury or disease." He met the patient's worried gaze with no warmth or reassurance in his tone. "No concussion. You'll be fine." Then, brusquely to Kim, "Clean him up."

Yeah, Doc, you can treat disease and injury, Paris thought as he watched the doctor-image reappear on the other side of a knot of wounded, snapping off emotionless commands to whatever hapless crewman stood nearby as he set to work. *It's just the treating the* patient *thing you've got to work on now.*

Janeway kept judiciously out of the way as Carey and one of his assistants activated the core seal with a great crack of thunderous light. Ozone seemed to blossom like fire in the air throughout the engine room. For one fearful moment, Janeway imagined that the warp-core leak had run wild, swallowing the ship, the crew, every bright hope for all their bright futures, in a single flare of atomic flame. Then the field's initial discharge settled into a deep, steady glow, and the nitrogen misting from the side of the core pinched off to nothing. She stared at Carey across a sudden weird, thrumming silence.

"Unlock the magnetic constrictors," she told him quietly.

Carey nodded and reached around his console to punch in the command. "Constrictors on-line."

Whatever sense of power coursed through the veins of a living ship swelled into life again. Their lives and deaths, all wrapped up in one matter-antimatter package. Janeway clenched one fist behind her back, a captain's prayer. "Pressure?"

"Twenty-five hundred kilopascals . . ." The engineer looked up from his instruments with a smile. "And holding."

Thank God, thank God! Relief washed over her in an almost fatiguing wave. Janeway flashed Carey a thumbs-up, and reached across to tap her comm badge when it beeped to interrupt them.

"Bridge to Janeway." Rollins's voice over the comm sounded brittle and laced with panic. "We're being scanned by the Array, Captain—it's penetrated our shields—"

Janeway turned her back on the engine room's bustle, trying to concentrate on the fading signal. "What kind of scan?"

She listened to blank air for nearly ten seconds before realizing it was silence she heard, not a pause.

"Bridge? Janeway to bridge! Respond!"

In the chill quiet that followed, the singing sparkle of a transporter crept up around her like a snake. Janeway whirled, and found Carey's horrified eyes through the fading silhouette of a young engineer. The boy was frozen in an atti-

tude of dull amazement as his atoms dispersed
into nothing

"Initiate emergency—!"

Without further warning, the alien transporter
beam caught her, choked off her breath, spirited
away her words. Janeway could only rage in frustrated silence as the engine room around her
dimmed, faded, and then was gone.

Sensors indicated contusions, edema, and development of a local subdermal hematoma. Suggested
treatment: An analgesic/anti-inflammatory regimen, in conjunction with application of cold packs
once the ship returned to noncombatant status.

"You're not seriously hurt," the patient was
informed as per Decision Track Number 30. "You
can return to your station."

Immediately, the transporter engaged and removed the patient from sickbay.

Upon query, sensors verified that no high-level
organic life remained within the sickbay. Decision
Track Number 1047 initiated manipulation of the
holographic interface to display a translatable facsimile of irritation. A channel to the bridge was
opened, and the vocalization subroutine reported,
"This is the emergency holographic doctor speaking. I gave no permission for anyone to be transported out of sickbay." Four hundred thousand
nanoseconds elapsed with no discernible activity
over the intercom channel. "Hello? Sickbay to
bridge."

Accidental Abandonment Subroutine self-activated one million seven thousand five hundred twenty nanoseconds later.

"I believe someone has failed to terminate my program," the vocalization subroutine informed the empty starship. "Please respond. . . ."

CHAPTER

7

SUNLIGHT SPARKLED OFF THE SURFACE OF A SMALL, clear pond, reflecting back through the weeping willows to dance around a summer sky as smooth and blue as a china bowl. On the big, sprawling white house, the shutters and porch rail were painted the same color, once upon a time. Through the years, though, sun, wind, and rain had finally faded the paint to a shade more like robins' eggs than sapphires. It was still a pretty effect, Paris decided, even if it had no place here, seventy thousand light-years from the very Terran Midwest it so chillingly resembled.

"Come up here . . . come on now . . ."

Paris jerked around, startled by the unfamiliar

voice, and nearly ran into Harry Kim as the ensign jumped in equal surprise while trying to carefully extricate himself from a rampant flower bed. There was crew all around them, Paris realized as he put out a hand to steady Kim. Scattered as far away as the barn and the tree line, some of them, but all apparently unhurt and unrestrained. At the foot of the house's long, wraparound porch, Janeway and a group of disoriented engineers milled in a small knot while a smiling, gray-haired woman in a flowered housedress and apron waved to them from the top of the stairs.

"I've got a pitcher of lemonade and some sugar cookies," she called cheerfully.

Tapping Kim on the elbow as a signal to follow, Paris jogged forward to join up with Janeway's small band. "Captain . . . ?" he began, then cut himself off. *What are you gonna ask? "Who is this lady?" "What're we doing here?" She's the captain,* he reminded himself, *not omniscient.*

Although, sometimes, good captains almost managed to be both. "Don't believe your eyes, Mr. Paris." Her own eyes flicked across the reading on her tricorder as the old woman on the porch waited with smiling patience. "We've only been transported a hundred kilometers—" Janeway looked at the old woman, then cocked her head upward with a thoughtful frown. "We're inside the Array."

Beside her, Kim passed his own tricorder over the porch stairs, the neatly trimmed grass. "There's no indication of stable matter. All this must be some kind of holographic projection."

Janeway nodded and slipped her tricorder back onto her belt. Above them, the hollow *clink-clunk* of ice dropping into tall glasses caught Paris's attention. The old woman clucked her tongue at him as she poured sun-colored liquid from a pitcher that hadn't been in her hands a moment before. "You poor things! You must be worn out. Sit down and rest awhile . . . have a cold drink . . ." She held out one of the tall, frosty glasses to no one in particular, tucking a wedge of yellow fruit onto the rim.

Janeway lifted both hands to politely refuse the offering. "No, thank you. My name is Kathryn Janeway, captain of the Federation *Starship Voyager—*"

"Just make yourself right at home." Still smiling, the old woman pushed the glass into the hands of one of the silent engineers, then wiped her fingers on the bib of her apron. "The neighbors should be here any minute." Something seemed to catch her attention behind them, and her smile widened. "Why, here they are now."

A swarm of chattering people swept over them without warning, pushing between crewmen, clasping hands, kissing cheeks. It felt like some sort of ludicrous family reunion where none of the members really knew each other. Paris found himself pinned between Kim and a young woman in blue-

and-white calico with hair the color of coal. "We're glad you dropped by," she told them with a shy smile. But the eyes she demurely averted seemed to imply she was anything but shy. Kim flushed but said nothing, and Paris felt himself return the girl's smile with a kind of stupid uncertainty that had nothing to do with pleasure.

"Now we can get started," the old woman announced with a clap of her hands. "You're all invited to the welcoming bee!"

A bent, gap-toothed old man with nothing but a wisp of frail white hair cackled and picked up a banjo. "Let's have a little music!"

Propping one foot up on the wooden steps, the old man stomped out a four-beat with his heel, then launched in with the banjo until it sang like a living thing. Standing shoulder-to-shoulder with Janeway and Kim, Paris watched the country folk dance and clap and laugh without feeling any urge to join in their festivities. *Well,* he thought, with a cynical wryness that had passed for his sense of humor over the last year, *it looks like we're not in Kansas anymore.*

Janeway paced to the corner of the long porch and back, decided she didn't like the nervousness that it might imply to whoever was no doubt watching, and sat instead on the wide porch steps with her hands wound together into a single fist between her knees. Out on the impossibly perfect lawn, their "hosts" had spread a patchwork quilt of colored blankets. Now they wandered placidly among the crew with bowls and platters of food balanced on their hands, inviting everyone to join them as if they were all old friends. Janeway had already instructed everyone to eat nothing, drink nothing, even though Kim still insisted that the tricorder said everything was a hologram and couldn't hurt them. Maybe so. But she didn't intend to take any chances.

Paris reappeared from around the back of the big red-and-green barn, jogging easily through the milling picnickers. In that fleeting moment of waiting —that necessary downtime between noticing Paris headed her way and standing for his actual arrival —Janeway almost forgot that he wasn't just any other crewman, assigned to *Voyager* from just any other ship. It was the absence of his smart-assed smile, she decided. All of a sudden, he was doing and thinking and being just like any other responsible adult, and it wasn't something Janeway had expected ever to see out of him.

You know what your problem is, Mr. Paris? she thought as he slowed to let Kim match his stride and approach the captain with him. *You aren't quite ready to trust you can make the right decisions, so you lash out at everybody who insists you work without a net.* Like Starfleet, his father, Janeway.

She had to admit, Paris had behaved admirably

on the bridge after the initial accident, when what needed doing was obvious and immediate. He'd seen to Stadi, reported his findings, kept his mouth shut, and kept out of the way. Likewise, the reassurance of following Janeway's straightforward commands right now seemed to calm him somehow—as though he was confident he could accomplish what she expected of him, and he was eager to prove that to her as well as to himself. She realized with a wry smile that labeling Paris as rebellious had been the biggest mistake Starfleet had made in his official record. He wasn't rebellious, he was unsure, and they'd cut him loose and made him an officer too soon. If they'd held him around as a noncom for just another two years, he probably wouldn't be here right now.

Which means none of us would be here right now. Janeway shook the thought away with an irritable sigh and pushed to her feet. No sense dwelling on any of the might-have-beens now. Just like Paris, she was going to have to make do with the way things were now, and not worry about how they could have been avoided "if only."

Paris and Kim joined her at the foot of the stairs, pulling together into a close circle so their voices wouldn't carry. "The crew's scattered around this farm, Captain," Paris reported, "but they're all accounted for."

That was something, at least. Janeway nodded and glanced around to take a quick count of who was in sight. "Move around," she told Paris and Kim. "Scan the area. See if you can find anything that might be a holographic projector."

"Have some fresh corn on the cob."

She jerked a look over her shoulder, startled by the nearness of the old woman's voice. Absurd as it was to expect she'd hear a hologram coming, Janeway still didn't like the thought of being so vulnerable around any group of people whose species she wasn't even sure of. She pushed Kim and Paris away from her, waving them on their way, and turned to place herself in front of the old woman as if that could prevent the hologram from following the younger officers if it wanted to. Old habits died hard. "Can you tell me why we're here?" she asked, ignoring the proffered plate of corn.

The old woman cocked her head, her incongruous smile never fading. "We don't mean you any harm—sorry if we've put you out. Just put your feet up and get comfortable while you wait."

She lifted the steaming plate toward Janeway again, and the captain gently pushed it aside, trying to keep frustration out of her frowning. "Wait for what?"

"Isn't anyone hungry?" the old woman called to no one in particular. She stepped around Janeway and held up her plate in gay exhibition. "Come now, make yourselves at home. Sorry to put you out . . ."

Apparently, the program—or whatever—wasn't

equipped to deal well with direct questions. Janeway slipped her tricorder from her belt to scan the woman's departure. Nothing new, but nothing useful, either. She closed the device up with a sigh.

Bounding out of the crowd, its silky coat floating around it like a cloud with every leap, a big puff of a dog galloped across the yard to bumble to its haunches in front of Janeway. She wasn't sure what engaged her more—the gray-and-gold coat and laughing eyes that reminded her so much of Bear, or the sloppy wet ball the dog dropped on her feet. A sudden throb of homesickness caught her by surprise. The thought of never seeing Bear, or Mark, or Earth again lay inside her heart like a lump of black glass, and reminded her with stinging force that this dog, this place, these people, weren't even real. Unlike the ones she'd left seventy thousand light-years behind her.

Picking up the soggy ball, she threw it toward a spot of open lawn without bothering to watch where it landed. The dog barked once with excitement, then tore off happily after its toy. Janeway turned her back on it, choosing instead to keep her heart and mind on her own people while she considered.

The dog barreled past them in a thunder of legs and hair and tail, nearly tripping Paris as it skidded frantically in front of him in pursuit of nothing particular that he could see. He watched it tumble to a stop a dozen meters beyond him, grinning stupidly at him through a face full of hair as it dropped a leather ball so wet and sloppy that it didn't even bounce. Paris could almost smell the pungent carnivore aroma of its breath all the way from here.

Why bother? he wondered as he looked at all the details incorporated into the shady animal's movements, smells, and sounds. Even the individual hairs inside its ears stirred as though feathered by a holographically suggested breeze. Alien holographic equipment must be delimited just like the human-built kind—held back by the sheer volume of data required to construct even the simplest simulation. Why bother expending the memory and processing capability needed to generate such fine detail in a noncommunicative element that could just as easily have been left out of the simulation altogether with no one being the wiser?

The dog popped a single excited bark, then snatched up its ball and bolted off again. Paris shook his head after it. *The whole point of calling them aliens,* he reminded himself, *is so we don't keep trying to understand and judge them by strictly human standards.* If that wasn't true of aliens from the opposite end of the Milky Way, then who else *could* it apply to? He pulled his tricorder off his belt and hurried after Kim as the younger man rounded the corner of the house just ahead of him.

Kim wasn't the only one waiting for Paris on the other side.

"The root cellar's right over there," the girl

volunteered with a smile. She pointed toward what looked like a slanted box made of two wooden doors on the ground a few meters away.

Kim immediately aimed his tricorder in the direction she indicated. "What's down there?" It occurred to Paris that Kim's naïveté was amazing.

"Potatoes . . . onions . . ." The girl linked her arm through Paris's and snuggled close to tip her head against his shoulder. "But it's real private. . . ."

I'll just bet it is. After all, it could be anything the hologram programmer decided it would be. The girl smiled up at him, real as life, and Paris had to admit that the spurt of hormones leaping through his system in response to her attentions felt equally heady and real.

Kim sighed and turned a shoulder to them both. "Paris, she's only a hologram."

He shrugged, ignoring the blush he felt creeping into his cheeks. "No reason to be rude." It was hard not to return a smile so sunny. Considering how much detail the aliens had invested in something as trivial to the scenario as a dog, Paris couldn't help wondering if they'd been just as meticulous with every aspect of their creations.

Kim's little bark of surprise distracted Paris from his musings. He pulled his attention away with a certain effort. "What?"

"Sporocystian life signs . . ." Kim thumbed through a series of readings on his tricorder, sweeping the area until he finally slowed to point at the sagging barn near the back of the property. "What's in the barn?" he asked the girl as he started forward.

"Nothing." She skipped after Kim with a bit more urgency than Paris had expected. "Just a big old pile of hay." He felt her fingers tighten on his arm, but whether to hurry him alongside her or to try to stop him from following, Paris couldn't tell. "C'mon . . ." she cajoled. "Let's go see the duck pond."

Why bother? The duck pond wouldn't be any more real than the barn, or the dog, or the girl. Kim's readings were probably the most tangible thing around at the moment. Suddenly, her touch and voice didn't gift Paris with quite the same thrill. He disengaged his arm from her grip, and moved up alongside Kim to distract himself with the blips and flashes racing across the ensign's tricorder screen.

"There's nothin' in there," the girl called from behind them. "It's just a dark, smelly barn."

But a barn that smelled more like ozone than animals, and whose wide-open door seemed to suck down light like a ravening black hole. Even as Paris watched, the lines of the building hardened and pulled in on themselves, sharpening the image into a knot of menace that only hid inside the shape of a barn. The levels on Kim's equipment shot skyward.

"You want some deviled eggs?"

Paris stepped inside the cavernous building without answering her.

It felt colder in here, somehow, and as dark as a grave despite the long slats of sunlight filtering between the boards of the walls. Something fractal and dusty lurked in a huge mound near the center of the structure, suspending a glitter of mist in the shadow-striped air above it. *Hay,* Paris realized with an odd little laugh. And the farm girl was right—it didn't smell very good.

He felt Kim move unconsciously closer, and Paris squinted at the ensign's tricorder as the girl tugged at his sleeve from behind. "See? Nothin' but hay."

Paris said nothing. Beside him, Kim lifted the tricorder and cocked his head with a frown.

"There's a life-form here," the ensign reported after a moment. "Just one."

Paris spared a glance for the "life-form" behind them. "Where?"

Kim turned slowly, his eyes locked on the readout as he swept the small sensor unit across the farm girl, the hay mound, the walls. "It's *every-where*," he said quietly. The tricorder sang as he aimed it beyond the pile of hay. "I'm also reading some kind of matrix-processing device. It may be the holographic generator—Paris!" Kim spun, dragging on Paris's arm as he waved the tricorder toward the barn's rear wall. "Humanoid life signs! Over here!"

A bolt of lightning seemed to explode through the building, smashing back the shadows. Paris ducked away from the flash, shielding his eyes with the crook of his arm, and felt Kim stumble back against him. On the tail of the blaze, a presence as heavy as thunderclouds swelled into being in front of them. Paris pushed Kim behind him, and squinted up at the farm girl as she materialized in their path, eyes aflame. "I'm not ready for you yet," she announced in an old man's gravelly baritone.

The dog's vicious snarl underscored her words, filling the darkness behind them. Paris heard Kim's yelp of surprise as he whirled to face the dog, and he slapped at his comm badge before his conscious mind had even pieced all the images together. "Paris to Janeway—!"

He didn't feel the blow that sent him flying— only heard the explosion of pain inside his skull when the farm girl's fist made contact, and saw the wave of darkness that crashed up to meet him as he fell.

She tapped her comm badge in response to the abortive shout. "Janeway here." Dancers and picnickers crowded around her, clapping in time to the banjo man's tangy playing. She turned her back on them, trying to grab some minimal quiet in the midst of all this artificial revelry. "Paris?"

Janeway didn't even let the silence stretch for as long as a minute before waving at the knot of engineers still gathered near the foot of the long porch. "Come on!"

Rounding the corner of the house, she heard the dog first—its basso roars cascaded out the open barn doors like the voice of a demon accidentally loosed from Hell. It reminded her absurdly of Bear's pointless fits whenever a delivery man passed too close to the house, and she was stung with an odd mixture of regret and fear. Then Kim's voice joined the dog's, sharp with alarm, and Janeway signaled the engineers to fan out as they burst through the doors and into the barn's dank interior.

For a moment, her eyes refused to adjust to the new dark. Snarls and banging rolled over her, directionless, and then the world seemed to snap into focus. She glimpsed Kim backed against an empty animal stall with the dog's teeth latched in his sleeve. And Paris, crumpled at the farm girl's feet and just starting to fight his way up to his knees. Janeway reached across her own front to brandish her phaser—then swallowed bitter frustration when she remembered that they were all weaponless, powerless, captured. The *boom!* of the barn door slamming behind them only solidified the helplessness of their position.

"Very well. Since no one seems to care for any corn . . ."

The voice belonged to the aging banjo man, but it was the grandmotherly woman from the house who flashed into existence barely inches from Janeway's face. Behind her, around her, everywhere, the rest of the scenario's farm folk appeared in the same eye blink, and the barn was suddenly crowded with them. Taking in their pitchforks and angry faces,

Janeway suffered a sudden urge to laugh at the tired cliché. Except these angry peasants had already proven themselves too dangerous to take so lightly.

"We'll have to proceed ahead of schedule," the old woman announced in the old man's voice.

Janeway opened her mouth to protest, to question, and found her voice frozen in her throat. Behind the ring of farmers, a low, pulsing hum built like a wave, dissolving the barn's rear wall as though it were the butter on the old woman's corn. Kim gasped and looked away, but Janeway made herself stare at the horror without blinking as she fought to memorize every detail, just in case any of them lived long enough to find the information useful.

A room longer than *Voyager*'s longest corridor extended past the back of the barn and into an unseen distance. Slabs hovered in neat, even rows along either wall, like examining tables in a monstrous mortuary, each holding a naked humanoid body. Tubes and wires and probes depended from the metallic ceiling to pierce the bodies below in more places than Janeway could count—like a life-support system, but with no life remaining in the subjects. Janeway tried to see what kind of fluids or gases passed through the tubes, but could only focus on the smooth, dark face of the Vulcan three beds away from her.

Light, as white and hurtful as a sun, blasted outward from the holographic farm folk. They shattered into silence and nothing, engulfing all sight and sound, eradicating the barn and everything in it until Janeway felt herself suspended, frozen, falling—

And then jerking back to awareness on her back. In the chamber. Staring upward at an array of probes and needles. Janeway tried to struggle, tried to twist aside as the first of the long implements slithered down toward her naked body with a deliberateness that seemed somehow both alive and frighteningly mechanical. Somewhere to her left, Kim screamed. *No!* her mind railed. *I won't allow this! They can't do this to my crew!*

Then the probe made its inexorable contact, cold metal against warm flesh, and pushed its way inside her chest despite all her pain and fear and anger. She didn't want to die for it—didn't want to give whoever controlled this awful funhouse the satisfaction of seeing her give up just because it could hurt her. But when the second probe burrowed in past bone and muscle to join its companion, she found that her body gave her no choice. Her mind crashed down into silence even as her soul still cursed their tormentor in every way it knew how.

CHAPTER
8

SHE CAME AWAKE NEATLY—WITHOUT FANFARE, WITH-
out trauma. As if someone had flipped a switch in
her brain. One moment she was aware of nothing,
and the next her eyes were open and the lights were
on and there was no jolt or fear or anguish between
the two. Pushing up to her knees, Janeway lifted her
head and looked around.

She was in Engineering. Carey and the rest of his
team lay scattered around the bay in roughly the
same positions they'd occupied before being
snatched, some of them sitting and waiting as
though unsure what to do, others crawling stiffly
upright as if just waking from some uncomfortable
sleep. Beside Janeway, the core seal enveloping the

warp drive hummed and glowed in placid oblivion. Just as if they hadn't left.

But Janeway knew that couldn't be true.

Climbing to her feet, she slapped at her comm badge as she moved to help Carey stand. "Janeway to bridge. Anybody there?"

"Yes, Captain." Rollins's voice sounded shaky, distracted. "We're here."

"How long were we over there?"

There was a delay during which Janeway assumed he checked his station's readout. She used the time to count the engineers in her sight and compare that number with her memory. "Almost three days," Rollins said just as she decided that everyone with her had apparently made it back in one piece. "Captain, the Maquis ship is powering up its engines."

"Tractor them!" Janeway returned Carey's questioning stare with a shake of her head, then headed for the turbolift as she signaled to every comm badge throughout the ship, "All senior officers, report to the bridge immediately!"

Paris recognized the sickbay the moment he opened his eyes. Crew members staggered to their feet from beside workstations, under examining beds. The medical drapes that had covered Fitzgerald and the dead nurse were neatly folded on a counter, but the bodies themselves were gone. The holographic doctor, he realized. The only one left behind when the alien Array evacuated *Voyager*. Turning, Paris scanned the crowded room for Kim as the doctor shifted its attention from a patient to materialize in front of Paris. "Could you explain what has transpired?"

No Kim. Not anywhere. Paris turned to answer the doctor as quickly as possible, then remembered he wasn't dealing with a real being when the hologram flickered aside in response to a patient's summons from across the room. He'd had enough of holograms to last anyone a dozen lifetimes. Turning his back when the doctor returned, Paris addressed the computer port at the nearest work-station. "Computer, locate Ensign Kim."

"Ensign Kim is not on board."

It hadn't even had to hesitate and search before giving its answer. Paris tapped his comm badge with a growing sense of panic. "Paris to Captain Janeway."

She responded almost as quickly as the computer. "Go ahead."

"Kim didn't come back with us. He must still be over there."

"Acknowledged." Something hissed softly beneath her stern voice, and Paris belatedly recognized it as the sound of a turbolift's doors when the busy cleanup noises of the bridge intruded on her next command. "Computer, how many crewmen are unaccounted for?"

"One," the cold machine voice answered. Paris

had already darted out the sickbay doors on his way to the bridge when it elaborated, "Ensign Harry Kim."

"Hail the Maquis."

Janeway tried not to fidget as Rollins fought with *Voyager*'s damaged systems to bring the comm unit on-line. Even so, she had to pace down to the main command level and position herself in front of the command chair just to wean enough frustration out of her system to keep from snapping at the big Native American who appeared on the screen. "Commander Chakotay, I'm Captain Kathryn Janeway."

His eyes narrowed. "How do you know my name?" Behind him, his own bridge was in shambles, one wall of consoles dead and burned as black as space. A dark-skinned officer, bent over one of the still-lit panels, glanced up at the sound of Janeway's voice, and she recognized the gentle wisdom of his eyes even before he stepped into the light to reveal his Vulcan features.

"We were on a mission to find you when we were brought here by the Array," Janeway told Chakotay, pretending not to notice the Vulcan behind him. "One of our crewmen is missing." She was pleased at how even and nonjudgmental her tone sounded. *He isn't the enemy,* she reminded herself about Chakotay. *Not anymore, not here.* It was easier to accept that now that she knew Tuvok was alive and undamaged among the Maquis crew. "Was he transported back to your ship by accident?"

Chakotay shook his head slowly. "No." Something very much like suspicion warred with uncertainty on his face; then the Maquis commander admitted with stiff unhappiness, "A member of our crew is missing, too. B'Elanna Torres, my engineer."

Janeway tried to imagine what a green Starfleet ensign and a Maquis engineer could have in common that an alien might want, but couldn't think of anything. "Commander," she said at last, "you and I have the same problem. I think it makes sense to try and solve it together, don't you?"

Chakotay snorted. "How can we . . ." He shook his head, not even trying to finish the thought.

"I'm fully aware that your crew is wanted for crimes committed in the Demilitarized Zone," Janeway told him, her frustration getting the upper hand. "But Chakotay, the Demilitarized Zone is thousands of light-years away. I don't think that means much right now, do you?"

He stared at her for a long moment, then glanced aside at Tuvok as though checking with the Vulcan before speaking out loud. Tuvok only lifted one eyebrow at his Maquis commander, and Janeway almost smiled at the familiarity of that gesture. When Chakotay turned back to her, he only nodded shortly. "Three of us will transport to your ship."

Then he cut the transmission before she could object.

Just as well, Janeway thought. *This keeps everything under my control.* She moved away from the center of the bridge, sparing only a quick nod toward Paris as he hurried out of the turbolift to join her beside the operations console. He looked downright subdued, she noted with some surprise. Maybe all the turmoil would prove to be good for him after all.

"They're powering down their engines," Rollins reported. "Dropping their shields."

Janeway stopped herself just short of ordering Rollins to do the same—it wasn't like *Voyager* had any shields to drop. A problem that would have bothered her a great deal more if Chakotay's ship were in much better condition. Turning to face the center of the bridge, Janeway moved to rest her hands on the railing and wait.

The itching tingle of a transporter beam diffused silently through the bridge, then pulled together into a hair-raising whine. As the first light of materialization swarmed the air in front of the shattered helm, Janeway stepped down beside her command chair to wait for the Maquis's atoms to stabilize before formally addressing them.

They solidified into three separate figures, Chakotay in the middle, each facing outward with his phaser drawn. Tuvok lowered his weapon the instant the transporter beam released him, but

Janeway still heard Paris swear quietly as a half-dozen members of *Voyager*'s crew pushed away from their stations to bring their own phasers to bear.

She spun to Rollins as the lieutenant started down toward her level. "Put down your weapons!" He hesitated, then flushed as though realizing he'd disobeyed a direct order, and slipped his phaser back onto his belt. Behind her, Janeway could hear Paris instructing the rest of the crew to do as they were told.

"You won't need those here." She waved at Chakotay's phaser, then waited.

It occurred to Janeway that the capacity for trust must be severely damaged in anyone truly dedicated to being Maquis. To be what you perceived as abandoned by the Federation, then hunted by Starfleet, and finally lied to and turned upon by the very people who fought beside you whenever a judicial plea bargain was made available. It raised her opinion of Chakotay even more, then, when after a moment of studying her and the crew surrounding her, he slowly holstered his phaser and motioned to his companions to do the same.

And it made it even harder to smile a welcome to the Vulcan without feeling that she was ruining what little ground she'd gained with the Maquis leader. "It's good to have you back, Tuvok."

Chakotay jerked as though stabbed, staring at the Vulcan. Lacing his hands behind his back, Tuvok turned to his Maquis captain and stated politely, "I must inform you that I was assigned to infiltrate your crew, sir. I am Captain Janeway's chief of security."

Chakotay looked as though he couldn't decide whether to be angry at the Vulcan or at himself. "Were you going to deliver us into their waiting hands, Vulcan?"

"My mission was to accumulate information on Maquis activities." But Tuvok inclined his head slightly in acknowledgment of the Maquis's statement. "And then deliver you into their 'waiting hands.' That is correct."

Chakotay clenched his jaw and his fists, and Janeway couldn't help wondering what he prevented himself from saying when he turned away from Tuvok with an angry growl. His dark eyes settled on someone behind Janeway's shoulder, and the angry color in his face gave way to cold hatred. "I see you had help."

"It's good to see you, too, Chakotay." Paris sounded glib and smug enough to slap.

"At least the Vulcan was doing his duty as a Starfleet officer," the Maquis spat. "But you . . . !" He gestured at Paris with undisguised loathing. "You betrayed us for what? Freedom from prison? Latinum? What was your price this time, *Poocuh?*"

Janeway didn't wait to see what effect Chakotay's words had on Paris's newfound self-respect. Stepping purposefully in front of the other commander, she planted a hand on his chest to warn him against moving any farther. "You're speaking to a member of my crew," she told him softly, evenly. "I expect you to treat him with the same respect you would have me treat a member of yours." When Chakotay took a grudging step backward, she lowered her arm and let him have the distance. He didn't seem quite able to take his gaze off Paris, though, and the pure hatred Janeway saw in his eyes disturbed her for all that it didn't much surprise her. "Now," she said, trying to pull the Maquis's attention back to what mattered. "We have a lot to accomplish, and I suggest we all concentrate on finding our people and getting ourselves back home."

Tuvok made his allegiance official by moving away from Chakotay to stand at Janeway's elbow. "Based on my initial reconnaissance, Captain, I am convinced we are dealing with a single entity in the Array. I would suggest that he scanned our computers in order to select a comfortable holographic environment. In effect, a waiting room—to pacify us, prior to a biometric assessment."

"An examination?" Paris asked.

Tuvok dipped a single nod—but to Janeway, not to this new crewman who had no functional rank. Janeway reminded herself to brief Tuvok on the situation later. "It is the most logical explanation," the Vulcan said. "Why else would we have been released unharmed?"

Paris gave a little snort. "Not all of us were."

Which brought them back to the real reason for their unsteady alliance. "Break out the compression phaser rifles," Janeway ordered Tuvok. "Meet us in Transporter Room Two. We're going back. We'll divide into two teams. Mr. Tuvok, while Chakotay and I look for Kim and Torres, your job is to find out as much about this Array as you can." She dared a frowning glance at the cloudy viewscreen and the alien structure that still dominated it. "It brought us here; we have to assume it can send us home."

As Tuvok led Chakotay and the other Maquis toward the turbolift, Janeway turned back to Rollins and the rest of her waiting bridge crew. "Mr. Rollins, maintain red alert. Keep us on constant transporter locks—"

"Captain?"

She stopped with one foot on the steps, burning to be out and doing, irritated at Paris's interruption. But when she twisted to look back at him, the simple bravery displayed on the young man's face caught her by surprise.

"I'd like to go with you," he stated simply.

A nanosecond flash of internal argument annihilated itself at the back of her brain. "If this has something to do with what Chakotay said—"

"It doesn't." Paris came up the steps to stand with her, his voice disarmingly sincere. "I'd just . . ." Something that was almost a blush moved across his features. ". . . hate to see anything happen to Harry," he finished awkwardly. But he met her measuring stare steadily, and there was none of his usual flippancy in his eyes.

Maybe not a waste after all. Janeway clapped him on the shoulder, nodding him toward the door as she sprang into motion again. "Come on."

CHAPTER

9

DUCKS STILL DRIFTED PLACIDLY ON THE MIRROR-BRIGHT surface of the holographic lake. Willows shushed in the warm summer breeze, and the sun hung precisely forty-five degrees above the gables of the blue-and-white farmhouse. Eternally a June mid-afternoon, just as they'd left here, only without the mercurial dog or the farm-folk revelers. Only the banjo-playing farmer remained, perched on the great porch's steps with his eyes closed as he plucked something eerily wistful out of the banjo's strings. Janeway wondered if the aliens in charge of this simulation had somehow identified this man and this house as the optimal soothing images for the current visitors, or if the holographic equipment involved was limited after all in how many patterns it could store and recombine for each new visit.

Tuvok opened his tricorder and released its song to drown out the banjo player's picking. "There are no humanoid life-forms indicated, Captain." He closed the device again. "Kim and Torres are not within tricorder range. They may not be on the Array."

Chakotay motioned at the banjo player with his compression rifle. *"He* can tell us where they are."

Yes, he very probably could. But Janeway wasn't so confident that they'd convince him to tell them. Shifting her own rifle to her left hand, she tapped the Maquis standing next to her and motioned him to join Tuvok. She didn't want the Vulcan wandering off without armed backup. "Maintain your comm link," she told Tuvok. "I don't want to lose anyone else."

The Vulcan nodded, then swept away with his tricorder open in his hand again, his head bent over the readings as though concerned with where his feet might go. Waving Paris and Chakotay to flank her, Janeway silently released the safety on her rifle before starting forward toward the house. She had no intention of using the gun unless forced to, but she wasn't about to be caught off guard anymore.

The hologram on the steps of the porch opened its eyes and stopped playing its half-senseless melody, then remarked, "Why have you come back? You don't have what I need."

Janeway swallowed an urge to slap the banjo out

of the hologram's hands. "I don't know what you need. And, frankly, I don't care. I just want our people back, and I want us all to be sent home."

"Well, now . . ." The hologram blinked at her with an old man's thin, patronizing smile. "Aren't you contentious for a minor bipedal species?"

"This minor bipedal species," Janeway snapped, "doesn't take kindly to being abducted."

It shrugged, turning back to its banjo. "It was necessary."

She felt Chakotay start to move more than saw it, and stopped the Indian's forward lunge with her elbow. To her surprise, he obeyed the silent command, but gripped her arm in unconscious frustration as he yelled at the hologram, "Where are our people?"

His volume had no impact. "They're no longer here."

"What have you done to them?" Janeway pressed.

"You don't have what I need," the hologram replied, as though answering some other question, or just refusing to answer that one. "They might." The strings on its instrument warbled unpleasantly, as though warping out of tune, but the hologram didn't seem to notice. "You'll have to leave them."

Chakotay shook his head. "We won't do that."

The melody twisted around itself to resolve back into something almost resembling music. Nodding its head to the rhythm, the hologram said nothing.

Janeway sighed and lowered her arm from in

front of Chakotay. "We are their commanding officers," she explained tightly. "We are entrusted with their safety. They are our responsibility. That may be a concept you don't understand—"

"No." For the first time, the eyes it turned upward at Janeway looked completely alive. Not a projection, not an image, but a real, living thing that suddenly exposed itself through the guise of this old country man. Janeway wanted to lunge forward and grab whoever this was before it faded away. "I do understand," the alien told her. "But I have no choice. There's so little time left."

Janeway held her breath for fear of shattering the rapport. "Left for what?"

"I must honor the debt that can never be repaid." It looked between their faces, its own expression bleak. "But my search has not gone well."

She glanced back at Paris and Chakotay, but saw only the same confusion in their eyes. "Tell us what you're looking for." She turned to face the hologram again with what she hoped it would recognize as open honesty. Or, at least, a facsimile of same. "Maybe we can help you find it."

"You?" It sniffed in amused derision—a frighteningly human sound. "I've searched the galaxy with methods beyond your comprehension. There is nothing you can do." Sighing, it looked down at its banjo, and Janeway noticed with a start that all the strings were broken. "You're free to go. If it's ever possible to return your people, I promise you I will."

"That's not good enough," Chakotay growled, and Janeway spoke over him in frustration.

"You've taken us seventy thousand light-years from our home! We have no way back unless you send us—and we won't leave without the others."

The hologram stood and hugged its banjo to its chest, staring off toward the duck pond and the swollen sun beyond it. "Sending you back is terribly complicated," it sighed. "Don't you understand? I don't have *time....*" The bright pond faded, swallowing the trees behind it, then the lowering sun, then the sky. *"... not enough time..."*

Then, somehow, before Janeway had fully registered the fading of the light or the disintegration of the landscape, brightness took over where the artificial world no longer stood—

And she was back on board the bridge of *Voyager*, facing the other four members of her landing party with no idea what to say to them, no idea what had brought them here.

No idea what to do.

He didn't hear their voices so much as feel them. *He's regaining consciousness ...*

Then the light flared painfully bright in front of his eyes, and Kim realized he was seeing it through his lids, burning through the pink tissue and black dreams. He flicked his eyes open, only to be instantly sorry when the brilliance burned past pain and seared the back of his skull. He wanted to tell them to move the light away, but couldn't force more than a hoarse moan past his lips.

Still, the brightness receded on the heels of his thought, and the pain washed aside as he blinked his vision clear.

A face swam suddenly into focus above him. *Above me?* He was lying on his back. The awareness came abruptly, like a lightning flash. He was lying on his back, on a bed, and he was cold. And the warm face bending over him belonged to a man he didn't know, a smooth, beautiful man who could have been young or old if not for the wealth of wisdom in his large eyes. He smiled at Kim, and asked gently, *How do you feel?*

Terrible, Kim thought. *I can't even see your lips move.* But he made himself take an unsteady breath and say, "What am I doing here? Where am I?"

Something very much like unhappiness flashed across the man's face, and he turned a look toward someone on his right. Kim followed his gaze, and saw a woman with the same indeterminate yet beautiful features. She took the man's shoulders and steered him away as she moved to stand beside Kim's bed.

It occurred to him without warning that he was in some kind of hospital. The smells—antiseptic yet sick—and the colors—heartless and drab— gave the place away as much as the overly calm and practiced behavior of this woman and all the others in the too-big room.

"Please, don't try to move yet." Her voice purred

pleasantly, but the intonations sounded false somehow, not quite right. "You are very ill."

"Ill?" He didn't feel ill. Confused, maybe. Frightened, yes. He pushed up onto his elbows and tried
to kick himself free of the ice-green sheets tangling
him to his bed. "There's some mistake," he tried
feebly to explain. "I'm not—"

Then he saw the thick knots of flesh distorting his
hand and arm, and his voice constricted into a tiny
cry.

What's wrong with me? Kim had never seen such
grotesque masses on anything still purported to be
alive. He jerked open the neck of his gown, found
even more thick swellings there, and had to blink
hard against the swirling darkness of shock when it
pressed the edges of his vision.

*What's wrong with me what's wrong with me
what's wrong—?!*

"No!"

The scream sounded human enough, although
the volume wasn't something Kim had ever heard
before. He jerked toward the painful sound just as
one of the quiet medical attendants crashed into a
table filled with equipment and shattered it to the
ground. A boil of movement exploded from where
the attendant had been, and a powerful figure leapt
over the downed man with no more effort than
Kim would have expended in swatting a fly. He
couldn't believe anyone could look so graceful in a
thigh-length hospital gown.

She whirled as if sensing him, and their eyes

locked for just a moment. *I know you!* Kim thought in stark surprise. He remembered her face—dark, big-boned, and brooding—on one of the slabs in the back of the holographic barn. Oh, God, that seemed like a century ago. She must be one of the Maquis. Which meant he wasn't here alone.

Or maybe everyone else but the two of them were *gone.* . . .

Kim didn't have a chance to ponder the details. Orderlies were suddenly filling the room, and the Maquis female nearly killed two of them fighting her way toward the door. She almost made it, too. But the attendant who had first smiled down at Kim and spoken without making the words wormed his way into the struggling knot of bodies with some unrecognizable device clutched in his hand.

Hold her still!

She howled like an animal, bucking underneath the combined weight of so many enemies. Then the smiling attendant—not smiling now, Kim noted grimly—reached past the wall of orderlies, and Kim heard the unmistakable hiss of a hypospray just before the Maquis fell still and silent at the bottom of the bundle.

The attendant heaved a groaning sigh and flopped back to the ground in evident relief. **Bring her over here,** he instructed as he climbed wearily to his feet.

Kim hugged the sheets against him as he watched the orderlies gather the unconscious woman with a gentleness that was almost bizarre. It wasn't their silence that held him riveted, or even the reverent care with which they now handled someone they had so mercilessly plowed to the ground only moments before. It was the coarse, ropy growths discoloring the Maquis's arms and neck that trapped his attention. That, and the very real knowledge that whatever was wrong with them might very well be what had happened to the rest of the crew. Which meant their chances of survival were not very good.

He wished their captors—caretakers?—had left him something more to wear than this gown and this blanket. Thinking of death with no one else here beside him, Kim suddenly found this dull alien hospital unbearably cold.

CHAPTER
10

"CAPTAIN'S LOG, STARDATE 48315.6 . . ."

Janeway cycled through the images on the data padd as it lay, unprotesting, on her desk. Picking it up seemed too much effort at such a late hour. Besides, that would require lifting her head off her other fist and actually sitting upright, which was not part of the bargain she'd made with her body for tonight. As long as she didn't require herself to be energetic and proper, her brain was allowed to stay functional long enough to file her last reports, review the damage and casualty lists, and decide everyone's role for the cleanup and repair teams tomorrow. So far, using one hand to tap at the controls had not been a violation of treaty, but she was fairly certain any movement approaching sitting up or standing would be. Scrubbing at her eyes, she forced her attention to divide again so she could finish her log and organize the repair details somewhat simultaneously.

"We've traced the energy pulses from the Array to the fifth planet of the neighboring system, and believe they may have been used in some fashion to transport Kim and Torres to the planet's surface."

The computer chimed, very politely, and she was forced to raise her head anyway so she could glance at the monitor for some sign of what she'd done wrong. Her words blinked placidly back at her. Janeway stared at them for nearly ten seconds before realizing that what she'd heard was the signal to the ready room's door, telling her that someone wanted in. Sighing, she sat back in her seat and made an effort to square her shoulders as she turned to face the entrance. "Come in."

Tuvok paused a painfully proper four steps into the room, his hands laced contritely behind his back. Over his shoulder, Janeway caught the briefest glimpse of the darkened, damaged bridge before the doors whisked shut and hid the image away. Had he been working out there all alone? This late at night? She wondered sometimes if Vulcans ever slept.

"Captain," he reported formally, "I have observed something peculiar about the pulses. They are getting faster."

She sat a little straighter. "Faster?"

Tuvok dipped a single nod. "The interval between each pulse has decreased by point-four-seven seconds since we arrived. I can offer no explanation."

She laughed a little—a dark, frustrated laugh that she didn't like the sound of much—and waved him forward to join her. "That's only one of the mysteries we're dealing with, Mr. Tuvok. Look at this." Turning her monitor to include them both, she leaned discreetly to one side so that Tuvok could bend over her shoulder without risking the unseemly possibility of physical contact. Janeway had heard rumors during her career about why Vulcans eschewed even casually touching humans, but had never been sure quite what to believe. All she knew was that Tuvok was always quietly consistent about maintaining what he considered an appropriate distance, and she had no intention of violating that.

He watched the planetary diagram spin beneath the glowing line of her words, the Array's dramatic flashes reduced by equations to little more than a series of short lines passing between *Voyager*'s current position and the planet's surface. Janeway reached up to tap the planet's statistics. "It's virtually a desert—the whole planet. Not one ocean, not one river." She sat back again, shaking her head. "It has all the basic characteristics of an M-class planet, except . . ." This time, she chose a particular string of figures out of the planet's description, and blew them up to fill nearly half the screen. ". . . there are no nucleogenic particles in the atmosphere."

Tuvok glanced down at her, one eyebrow arched. "That would mean the planet is incapable of producing clouds and rain."

Janeway nodded, chewing her lip. "I've studied thousands of M-class planets—I've *never* seen an atmosphere without nucleogenics. There must have been some kind of extraordinary environmental disaster." A yawn captured her suddenly, and she hid it behind a vigorous face scrubbing. "As soon as repairs are complete," she continued when her voice was back, "we'll set a course for the fifth planet."

"Captain, you require sleep."

She felt a blush push into her face—embarrassment at being caught in a lie, frustration at being caught in weakness—and reached for her waiting data padd without looking up at the Vulcan's calm face. "Kim's mother called me just after he left Earth . . . a delightful woman . . ." She paged through the data in front of her blindly. "Her only son." The words were even harder to say than to think. "He'd left his clarinet behind, and she wanted to know if she had time to send it. . . . I had to tell her no." She glanced up at Tuvok without meaning to. "Did you know he played clarinet in the Juilliard Youth Symphony?"

Tuvok said nothing for a moment. Then, "I did not have the opportunity to meet Mr. Kim."

It sounded so final when he said it that way. As though he knew he'd never have the chance now. "I barely knew him," Janeway admitted. "I never seem to have the chance to get to know any of them. I have to take more time to do that." It was a good promise, one she knew she'd made to herself before this, on other ships, with other crew. "It's a fine crew," she said out loud, defensively. "I've *got* to get them home."

"The crew will not benefit from the leadership of an exhausted captain," Tuvok pointed out with his traditional patience.

Janeway couldn't help but smile, just a little. "You're right. As usual." She sat back in her seat and sighed up at him. "I've missed your counsel, Tuvok."

He inclined his head in acknowledgment. "I am gratified that you came after me so I can offer it once again."

It was so close to a Vulcan admission of feelings, Janeway wasn't entirely sure what to say. She'd once read a quote from a famous admiral that said, "Friendship with a Vulcan is like sculpting with radioisotopes. Very few people ever try it, and the ones who do have a hard time explaining how the milliseconds of closeness when it all comes together can make such an experiment worthwhile." Sometimes, staring into the darkness of Tuvok's calm expressions, Janeway found herself thinking that the admiral should have warned her that those daring few who forged friendships with Vulcans didn't exactly choose to follow that path—it happened without your planning in the first millisecond flash when you looked into a Vulcan's eyes and realized that he understood that you had feelings, and vice versa.

Caught by her own overlong silence, Janeway said, "I spoke to your family before I left."

A human would have reacted. Tuvok only asked, "Are they well?"

"Well," Janeway told him. "But worried about you."

One of many Vulcan nonexpressions—most of which stood in for more human displays of annoyance, disgust, or impatience—ghosted across Tuvok's face. "That would not be an accurate perception, Captain. Vulcans do not 'worry.'"

Or feel gratitude. "They miss you," she amended.

That seemed to suit him better, although what passed through his eyes was a simple tenderness Janeway wasn't accustomed to seeing there. "As I do them."

"I'll get you back to them." The statement blurted out of her, as unexpected and honest as Vulcan friendship, and Janeway felt the words burrowing in to stay even as she spoke them. "That's a promise, Tuvok."

He accepted it as stoically as he would any other truth. Janeway smiled wearily, and watched as the Vulcan nodded his good-night and retreated through the ready-room door. Now if only she could believe herself so easily.

CHAPTER
11

FIVE HOURS LATER, SHE WAS NO CLOSER TO BELIEF—OR sleep—than when Tuvok first left the ready room.

I probably should have gone back to my quarters. Even a starship's bunk was more comfortable than a couch that Janeway suspected was constructed more for the sake of its appearance than for its usefulness. But her quarters held what was left of her unpacked luggage, the two articles of civilian clothing she had brought to remind her of autumn back home, the pictures of Mark and darling Bear. She'd learned long ago that while guilt can be a great motivator, it can also be a great destroyer—it thrived on stolen energy.

An innate awareness of this fact no doubt had something to do with why, somewhere between shutting down the screens and killing the lights last night, she'd been overwhelmed with the conviction that a return to her quarters would somehow represent a surrender. That by going to bed the way she would have on any other day of her career, she was accepting that this was how she would be going to bed from now on—that this was *where* she would be going to bed, with no hope of ever seeing a real home again. So she'd stretched out on the hard, aesthetically pleasing gray couch and draped one arm across her eyes, and told herself that she was just being efficient by sleeping so close to the bridge. In case she was needed.

Five hours into her nonsleep vigil, she knew that there were seven primary welds in the ready-room ceiling, and that the bridge air-recirculation system turned on an average of twice every hour.

I should have gone down to sickbay and had that holographic medical program anesthetize me.

She should have made sure Mark understood that every mission meant a chance the captain might not come home when she asked him to watch Bear while she was gone.

She should have said no when Starfleet asked her to head up this assignment.

Growling with frustration, she rolled onto her shoulder and covered her face in her hands, trying to grind away the insidious should-haves with the pressure of her fists against her eyes.

Her comm badge chirped and saved her from further self-anger. "Bridge to Captain Janeway."

Apparently, Tuvok really didn't sleep. "Go ahead." She tried to sound rested and alert, but knew she failed miserably.

"Sorry to bother you, Captain." Tuvok's eloquent way of letting her know he could interpret human tone of voice even if Vulcans chose not to emulate them. "But we've encountered a vessel within a debris field. We're showing a humanoid life-form on board."

"On my way." She rolled to her feet and ran her hands back through her hair. *I may not look presentable, but at least I can look driven.* She slipped through the door to the bridge while it was still only halfway open. "Hail them."

Rollins turned toward the ops station to comply, and Janeway moved to the foot of the command station to study the image on the main viewscreen. A vast scattering of ships glittered and tumbled among what could only be satellite debris and the remnants of wrecked probes. A squat, dish-decorated cylinder that looked like nothing so much as Earth's earliest Martian probe drifted behind the skeletal remains of an Exian freighter whose cargo had long since eaten its way through the hull. The thought of there being any sort of humanoid life still living in this dark, silent sargasso chilled her.

The screen brightened abruptly, and a small, dome-headed alien with eyes a strikingly chocolate brown announced, "Whoever you are, I found this waste zone first."

Janeway allowed herself a slight smile. Judging from his stooped shoulders and awkwardly raised chin, there was only so much dignity one could adopt when squeezed into a cabin not even as tall as yourself. "We're not interested in this debris, Mister . . ."

He seemed to understand her expectant pause. "Neelix." He introduced himself with a flare of his arms that rapped his knuckles against either wall. "And since you aren't interested in my debris—" A delightful smile split his hairless features. "—I am delighted to meet you."

"Captain Kathryn Janeway," she replied, more formally, "of the Federation *Starship Voyager.*"

Neelix granted her a courtly nod. "A very impressive title. I have no idea what it means, but it sounds very impressive." He smiled again, and Janeway wondered if he made an effort to sound so eager and funny, or if everyone of his race approached the world with such puppy-dog enthusiasm.

If she had her way, *Voyager* wouldn't be in this end of the universe long enough to learn the answer.

"Do you know this area of space well, Mr. Neelix?"

"I am famous for knowing it well," he assured her proudly. "How may I be of service?"

She avoided extending a specific request for the moment. "Do you know anything about the Array that's sending energy pulses to the fifth planet?"

An odd, tittering giggle squinted his eyes shut. "I know enough to stay as far away from it as possible." Calming himself, he blinked rapidly as though to clear all the mirth from his vision, then said brightly, "Wait. Let me guess." Somehow, the soft congeniality never seemed to completely leave his tone and eyes. "You were whisked away from somewhere else in the galaxy, and brought here against your will."

Janeway felt a strange stirring of dread deep inside her. "It sounds as though you've heard this story before."

"Sadly, yes." Neelix sighed. "Thousands of times." Then he shrugged and admitted, "Well, hundreds—maybe fifty times." His preoccupation with accuracy scattered with a wave of his hand. "The Caretaker has been bringing ships here for months now."

Tuvok made not a sound, but Janeway sensed the sharpening of his curiosity and waved him to stay silent. "The Caretaker?"

"That's what the Ocampa call him. They live on the fifth planet." Neelix leaned forward as though trying to crawl through the viewscreen, but was only rearranging himself on the floor, Janeway realized. She spared a fleeting thought about who —or what—had originally piloted that tiny vessel. "Did he kidnap members of your crew?" Neelix asked.

She sniffed a cynical laugh. "As a matter of fact, he did."

Neelix bobbed his head in sympathy. "It's not the first time."

"Do you know where he might have taken them?"

"I've heard they're sent to the Ocampa," Neelix told her. "Nothing more."

It was more than they'd had before. "We'd appreciate any help you could give us in finding these Ocampa."

Neelix cocked his head as though listening to someone who wasn't really there, the sadness in his eyes warring with the curiosity of his hands on the lifeless equipment in front of him. "I wish I could help," he sighed, "but as you can see, there is so much debris to investigate today." He leaned forward again, this time in friendly confidence. "You'd be surprised the things of value some people abandon."

If he'd been a Ferengi, she'd have been more sure that feral glimmer was entirely motivated by greed. Following her instincts, she offered sweetly, "Of course, we'd want to compensate you for your trouble."

The expression of utter innocence that flashed across his face convinced her even further that, wherever Neelix came from, his people had obviously escaped from the more moderate Ferengi generations ago. "There's very little you could offer me," he assured her earnestly. "Unless . . ."

He was doing all right until that qualifier. "Yes?" Janeway prompted.

"Unless," he repeated in the same oh-so-speculative tone, "of course, you had . . ." Dark eyes brightened eagerly. "Water."

She knew the surprise showed on her face, compounded by the fact that an instant later she didn't know why such a request had even startled her. The closest habitable planet—and Neelix certainly wasn't going very far, very fast in any of the rotted hulks around them—didn't even have enough surface water to support a brown savannah. That meant what she took for granted every morning in her coffee was probably the most valuable bargaining tool she could have hoped for. "If you help us find our missing crew members, you can have all the water you want."

Neelix dropped his jaw in dumb amazement, then jerked it shut with a snap too late to disguise the reaction. "That seems like a . . ." He stammered trying to find the words. ". . . reasonable arrangement."

More than reasonable, and Janeway had the advantage of knowing it. "Good. We'll beam you over and tow your ship into our shuttlebay." She had a feeling the little wreck wouldn't survive a tractor beam's stress without blowing every atmosphere seal. "Mr. Tuvok, go to Transporter Room Two and meet our guest."

Neelix shifted uncertain eyes between Janeway and the Vulcan's retreating back as Tuvok turned without comment for the turbolift. "Beam?" Neelix squeaked uncertainly.

Janeway lifted an eyebrow. So transporter technology wasn't the norm among spacefaring worlds on this side of the pond. That was something worth keeping in mind. "We have a technology which can take you instantly from your ship to ours. It's quite harmless," she hurried to assure him when something that might be either excitement or terror crossed his face. "May we?"

He lifted his arms in acceptance, marvelous wonder still lingering on his face as the transporter reduced him to sparkling atoms and ghosted him away.

The first thing Tuvok noticed about their guest was his smell.

He might have postulated that Neelix's people exuded a protective musk, like toadlets on Rudolpha IV. Or even that the glandular secretions from Neelix's reproductive endocrine cycle only registered as unpleasant to a Vulcan's hypersensitive nose, while smelling positively sensual to members of his own species. Like Klingons, or certain humans at certain points in their development. Tuvok might even have been willing to exercise that peculiar human custom Benefit of the Doubt and construct a working hypothesis based on Neelix's recent exposure to a derelict vessel of unknown origin and dubious ventilation. But then Neelix straightened out of his nervous crouch and stumped down the steps to stand less than an arm's length from Tuvok, and the Vulcan was forced to

Captain Kathryn Janeway (Kate Mulgrew) on the bridge of the *U.S.S. Voyager.*

Tom Paris (Robert Duncan McNeil) and Ensign Harry Kim (Garrett Wang) come on board the *U.S.S. Voyager.*

In the *Voyager*'s sickbay, the holographic medical program (Robert Picardo) is called into action when the crew loses its regular medical team.

Maquis commander Chakotay (Robert Beltran), Captain Janeway, and Tom Paris try to get some answers from the enigmatic Caretaker (Basil Langton).

Half-Klingon, half-human Maquis Engineer B'Elanna Torres (Roxann Biggs Dawson) is held in stasis by the mysterious "banjo man."

In an Ocampa hospital, Ensign Harry Kim is shocked by the strange growths erupting on his body.

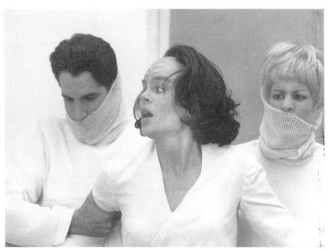

B'Elanna Torres struggles to escape from an Ocampa hospital.

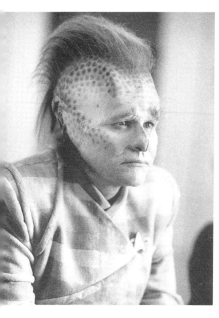

Neelix (Ethan Phillips), a friendly Delta Quadrant denizen, offers his services to Captain Janeway in return for water.

Searching for answers, Tuvok (Tim Russ), the *Voyager*'s Vulcan Chief of Security, scans the abandoned farmyard in the Array.

Captain Janeway confronts the Caretaker with the flaws in his thinking.

Neelix, Tom Paris, and the Ocampa alien Kes (Jennifer Lien) work together to rescue Ensign Kim and B'Elanna Torres.

The Kazon-Ogla: the new enemy.

Captain Janeway and Chakotay, her new first officer, prepare the crew for the long journey home.

admit that every last molecule of stench emanated directly from Neelix and the skittering insectile menagerie that scrambled for cover beneath the alien's equally stink-drenched clothes.

Tuvok coughed politely into his palm.

"Astonishing!" Trundling around behind Tuvok, Neelix bobbed up onto his toes to wave cheerily at the transporter technician behind the transparent protective barrier. "You Federations are obviously an advanced culture."

Tuvok turned to watch the little creature's curious progress around the transporter room, but found himself unable to willingly step any closer. "The Federation is made up of many cultures. I am Vulcan."

"Neelix." The alien spun, thrusting out a hand in an exuberant offer of friendship. "Good to meet you."

The thought alone of touching skin that both smelled and crawled forced another little cough out of Tuvok. That tiny breach in his Vulcan discipline so startled him—yet another inappropriate reaction, his cool inner voice informed him—that he didn't even have time to be grateful that Neelix was too quickly distracted to insist that Tuvok shake hands. Tuvok held his ground, reciting each stanza of the calming *Pok'Tow* in his head, as Neelix scurried across the room again to poke at an intercom panel with one dirty finger.

"Interesting. What exactly does all this do?"

"I assure you—" It took every ounce of his

Vulcan control to step politely forward and gesture Neelix toward the transporter-room door. "—everything in this room has a specific function. However, it would take several hours to explain it all. I suggest we proceed to your quarters." He was so pleased by Neelix's willingness to precede him out into the corridor that he added smoothly, "Perhaps you would care for a bath."

Neelix blinked up at him earnestly. "A what?"

For the first time, Tuvok experienced something close to regret that Janeway had successfully rescued him from the Maquis.

CHAPTER
12

KIM HAD AWAKENED THAT MORNING FEELING COLD, lonely, and just a little bit sick. The first two he attributed to being held hostage in a colorless alien hospital with nothing to wear but a light cotton robe, and no one he knew to depend on or talk with. The one time he'd been hospitalized as a child—for exposure to Rigellian fever after playing Starfleet explorer with a passel of rambunctious green children from an Orion diplomat's entourage —his mother and father had hovered about his quarantine suite the entire time. He hadn't even felt sick then (he never did get around to developing symptoms), but he'd still had all the books and films any boy could have wanted to drive boredom away, and Mother had even brought him his clarinet, in case his stay expanded to something longer than a week. As it was, he'd been allowed to go home after only three days, and his mother still threw him a "welcome home" party and invited all his friends.

Just remembering her round, happy face in comparison with all this dullness pushed a fresh clot of loneliness into his heart, and Kim had rolled over on his cold alien cot and cried quietly to himself until the worst of it went away.

Now, the silence of the dim infirmary only exacerbated the sick weakness in his stomach. Like an old analog clock, whose ticking both kept you awake and forcibly reminded you of the winks you were missing. Sitting up, he tried to adopt an air of professional calm as he tugged wide the collar of his gown and peeked down it to inspect the knobby growths he'd already examined some five or six other times since first waking up in this strange setting. A shaky little sigh escaped him. "Still there," he whispered to himself wryly. The rest of him couldn't seem to think up a clever reply.

The rash of warty flesh didn't seem to have spread, but, then, Kim hadn't been able to conduct any sort of systematic study with only the occasional peek now and then. It sort of fell into the category of "didn't want to know." He felt a little guilty about that—he couldn't help thinking Paris would have owned up to every ounce of the unpleasantness, and even made a joke about it, to boot. But Kim could only finger these unfamiliar additions to his arms and chest and neck, and wail somewhere deep inside himself, *I'm only just an ensign! I'm not supposed to die—not yet!* Honest, perhaps, but far from very helpful.

A groggy snarl from the other side of the infirmary snagged his attention, and Kim froze with his gown bunched up in his fist, glancing nervously toward the sound. He listened tensely for a moment, then relaxed with a silent laugh when the broken cry sounded again and he recognized the voice as coming from the swarthy Maquis who had tried so desperately to escape the night before. *Hell, I probably wouldn't know what she sounded like if she actually* talked! She'd certainly been vocal enough up to now, although not exactly communicative.

Swinging his legs over the edge of the bed, Kim tossed a quick glance toward the closed infirmary door before padding barefoot across the cold floor to the only other occupied bed in the room.

She lay as stiffly as if she were struggling, even with the alien knockout drug still tying her to drowsiness. Kim thanked his own better instincts that he hadn't exploded, too, upon first coming around; if he had, both of them would be fighting their way toward consciousness, not just her. He studied her dark face and ridged brow, and wondered what bloodlines had carved such permanent fury into her face, painted such a dark luster through her raven-black hair.

"It's okay. . . ." A waft of chilly air hiked up the

back of his gown, and Kim reached back to clutch it shut as he sidled a little closer to her shoulder. "It's okay," he soothed.

The Maquis jerked upright with a horrified gasp. Kim jumped back, suddenly glad he hadn't tried to touch her, and found himself meeting her accusing glare with what he was sure was a look of stunned utter innocence. "Who are you?" she hissed, kicking her blankets aside. "What is this place?" The growths on her arms and neck were more livid and extensive than his own.

Kim, his hand still knotted in the gown behind his back, shrugged and offered what he hoped was a reassuring smile. "My name is Kim—Harry Kim. I'm an ensign on the *Starship Voyager.* I was kidnapped from the Array, just like you." He glanced around at the primitive room. "I don't know where we are," he had to admit.

She surged out of her bed with the power of a young lion, and set out across the room as though fixed on a purpose Kim could only surmise. "What was Starfleet doing at the Array?" she demanded as she swept the closest table clear of debris.

"We were looking for you, actually." Kim watched her prowl from bed to table, table to wall, and realized that what he'd taken for direction was nothing more than frustration screaming for a way to get out. "One minute, we were in the Badlands. The next . . ." He threw his arms wide for lack of any better way to express their predicament, and his gown flapped open again.

Just as inelegantly dressed as Kim, the Maquis seemed unmoved by his half-clad state. She ripped a drawer half off its runners and pawed through the clutter inside. "You mean you were trying to capture us."

"Yeah." Considering the results, Kim couldn't help smiling dryly at the irony. "Consider yourself captured." He made a show of patting around at his skimpy gown. "I know I have a phaser here somewhere."

The Maquis glared at him before beelining for the only door. "I don't find this at all amusing, Starfleet."

He had a feeling she didn't find much amusing. Too bad. She might almost be pretty if she ever smiled.

"There's no point," Kim said when she started tugging at the door handle with both hands. "It's locked." He'd already tested it twice before during one of his other wakeful phases.

She pushed him aside when he tried to move in front of her, and Kim could tell by the bunching of the muscles in her jaw that she had no intention of letting something like a locked door or some strange tumors keep her in confinement. "Hey . . ." He caught at her wrist as she pounded first her hands, then her elbows and feet against the door with increasing violence. "Hey! What's that going to accomplish?"

She was stronger than he expected, and nearly slammed him to the ground when he suspected all she meant to do was shrug him away. Her hands clenched into white-knuckled fists to shower the door with a thunder of blows. *"What are they doing to us?! What are these* things *growing on us?!"*

Kim stayed very still on the ground, a little afraid to confront her. "Do you want them to sedate you again?" he asked, very reasonably.

To his surprise, she jerked a look at him as though not realizing he was still there. Then anger, embarrassment, and anger again chased each other across her dark face, and she whirled away from the door to pace in time with her growling breaths. "You're right, Starfleet," she admitted in a lower but no less bitter tone. "It's the Klingon half of me. I just can't control it sometimes."

Klingon. That explained both the strength and her exotically darkened features. Kim climbed carefully to his feet to follow her across the infirmary. "What's your name, Maquis?"

She flicked a glare at him as though not sure if she was being made fun of, then seemed to dismiss the thought with a shake of her head. But she answered, "B'Elanna. B'Elanna Torres," in a voice that was almost civil. She stopped to rend a sheet with her hands. "Have they told you anything?"

Kim thought about taking the fabric away from her, decided better the sheet's destruction than his own. "Only that they're called the Ocampa. I can tell you one other thing—their medicine is from the Dark Ages." He boosted himself onto the bed across from her. "The nurse actually tried to bleed me this morning."

That at least wrung a smile from her. Funny the kinds of things Klingons found amusing. He answered her with a friendly grin of his own, and let her savage the bedclothes for a few more minutes in companionable silence.

At first, Kim's subconscious didn't recognize the soft clunk behind him as a sound that should alarm him. He was too used to Starfleet doors that whisked open on a sigh to hear the subtle movement of latches and hinges. Torres, however, stiffened like an animal at the first quiet *snickt!* She dropped the sheet in a tangle of fraying thread, and Kim jumped down from the bed to grab her elbow when she tensed in readiness to run. *Don't!* he mouthed, praying that her Klingon half would stop and listen to his human-inspired reason. God knew he couldn't very well stop her if she decided to bolt.

Breathing hard, her teeth clenched, Torres nodded stiffly without taking her eyes off the door. A minor victory, but enough. Tightening his fingers on her arm in combined encouragement and warning, Kim turned slowly to follow her gaze.

The Ocampa in the doorway stood with his arms folded around a bundle of gray-green fabric, his delicate lips stretched into a warm yet somehow infuriating smile. *The doctor,* Kim remembered. Or, at least, the robed attendant whose gentle voice had first reached past Kim's confusion to soothe him with uncertain words and stilted sentences. As though hearing Kim's thoughts across the tense distance, the doctor found the ensign's eyes and nodded warm acknowledgment, relaxing visibly. "I hope you're feeling better," he said aloud, his voice still slow and oddly inflected. "I know how frightening this must be for both of you. I've brought you some clothes, if you'd care to change." He extended the bundle of cloth in his hands, as though only just remembering he had it there.

Torres trembled with frustration under Kim's grip. "Why are you holding us here?"

The Ocampa's eyes flew wide with surprise. "You're not prisoners. In fact—" He moved carefully forward, clothes still outstretched. "—we consider you honored guests. The Caretaker has sent you to us." He looked meaningfully at Torres as he passed the new clothes across the bed between them. "As long as you're not violent, you're free to leave your quarters."

Quarters. What an interesting study in the power of language when a room can go from hospital to containment cell to quarters all in the span of a single day. Kim held out his arm to display the discolored growths littering his skin. "What's wrong with us? What *are* these things?"

"We really don't know," the doctor admitted, obviously uncomfortable with the question. Brightening somewhat forcibly, he continued, "You must be hungry. Would you care to join me in the courtyard for a meal?"

The very mention of food clutched at Kim's stomach with hunger. It had been a long time since he had even smelled the holographic corn bread at the Array's family picnic. He stole a glance at Torres, and found her looking a bit wistful, too, at the suggestion. "Give us a minute to change," he told the doctor. The Ocampa nodded agreeably, and scampered back out the door.

"I think he's lying," Torres announced the moment they were alone again.

Kim laughed wryly as he shook out a pair of loose trousers and held them in front of him for size. "Lying? About what? He hasn't even *told* us anything yet."

"About our being free to go." She managed to make even that simple statement sound like an epithet. Turning her back to Kim, she tore off her gown and started shrugging into a long tunic. "About not knowing what's wrong with us." She paused to stare down at herself in dour reflection. "If they didn't do this to us, then who did?"

"Maybe nobody." Kim passed her the second pair of trousers and waited while she stepped into them. "Maybe we just picked up something."

Torres growled what was either an oath or an animal snarl. "I don't like him."

I never said I liked him, Kim thought. But he left Torres to her private steaming as he led the way out into the hall.

The doctor greeted them with a broad grin, but stopped himself just short of touching them. In a flash of pointless memory, Kim knew the Ocampa's hands would be warm, and deliciously gentle. He shook the image off with an effort.

"I'm so happy to see you up and about," the doctor assured them. He waved them down the dim, unadorned hallway, then fell into step beside Kim. "Treating visitors is always difficult, no matter how careful and clever we try to be."

Kim exchanged a look with Torres. She made a face, obviously remembering the same archaic treatments as he. "If we're not prisoners," Kim told the doctor in as friendly a tone as possible, "we'd like to return to our ships and our own doctors."

A sorrowful expression melted across the doctor's face. "That isn't possible. You see, there's no way to get to the surface."

Torres impaled him with a dark glare. "What do you mean, 'to the surface'?" But Kim saw the answer even as the words came out of her mouth, and the doctor stayed wisely silent as they stepped from the dreary tunnel into the greater light of artificial day.

The city stretched farther than Kim could see, arching gradually downward until it disappeared beneath a horizon closer than any surface planetary horizon Kim had ever seen. Walkways and ramps and mechanized stairways glittered back and forth between the spare buildings—like webs, spun by the drifting antigrav platforms, to hold the weary place together beneath the great weight of stone and earth that formed the sky above it. Even the people dotting the scene seemed tired and worn. They rode the sliding walkways as though not interested in finding their own ways to destinations, the uniform noncolor of their clothing in odd contrast to the studied differences carefully built into each of their outfits. Kim wondered if the addition of birds, or trees, or grass, or flowers would help the place look more alive. Probably not. The lack of spirit rested in the quiet conformity with which the Ocampa went about their small, cheerless duties. Besides, whatever painted the pale, bluish light across this cavelike world wasn't a singular source—it probably didn't produce enough radiant energy to keep algae alive.

"We're underground . . ." Kim meant to say something more meaningful, but couldn't stop the amazed exclamation from escaping.

The doctor nodded, apparently understanding of the ensign's surprise. "Our society is subterranean. We've lived here for over five hundred generations."

"But before that—" Torres must have heard the same unfinished longing in the doctor's tone. "—you lived on the surface?"

He nodded. "Until the Warming began."

"The warming?" Kim asked.

"When the surface turned into a desert, and the Caretaker came to protect us." Cutting himself off, the doctor stepped down toward one of the many moving walkways, but stopped before actually mounting it. He glanced back as though expecting them to follow, and Kim tugged impatiently at Torres's arm. He was hungry for answers even more than for food, and was glad when the Maquis came along without protest. The doctor smiled as they caught up to him, then led the way deeper into the sterile city.

"Our ancient journals tell us he opened a deep chasm in the ground," he explained, looking at the Ocampa passing around them instead of directly at his patients, "and led our ancestors to this place. He has provided for all our needs since then."

Which didn't include the infusion of much brightness or color, as near as Kim could tell. And if the place had been any more silent, it would have made Kim want to scream. Leaning around Torres, he tried to see beyond the nearest archway for some sign of people congregating, socializing, talking, and found himself facing a small crowd of Ocampa who stared back at him with frank curiosity. They touched each other and glanced among themselves as though exchanging the same gossip and niceties as any other social gathering, only silently. So silently.

"Please forgive them." The doctor moved in front of Kim with a bobbed apology, shooing the spectators on their way. "They know you've come from the Caretaker. None of us has ever seen him." He hesitated as the knot of people gradually cleared, revealing a softly lighted plaza crissed and crossed by a long queue of patiently waiting Ocampa. "Oh." The doctor raised up on tiptoe to see across the quiet gathering. "I'm afraid one of the food dispensers has failed again. The service attendant must be busy elsewhere." Pushing gently through the chain of people, the doctor startled Kim with the sound/feeling of his voice the way Kim had first experienced it the day before. *Would you please excuse us?* Maybe the silence in this underground city wasn't so unhealthy for the Ocampa after all.

All around them, people glanced up as the doctor's words touched them, their pale faces turning toward Kim and Torres like flowers toward a distant sun. Kim returned their wondering stares with a nervous smile, feeling oddly guilty for their attentions. When he and Torres reached the front of the line, the doctor reached around the first Ocampa in the queue and lifted the door to an innocuous wall unit so he could slide out two trays of moist, textureless food. It look distressingly like dog food, and it smelled like nothing much at all. Kim wrinkled his nose but didn't comment, and passed one tray along to Torres as the doctor darted forward to liberate a third from the open dispenser unit. The trays, the utensils, even the lumpy mounds of processed protein, could have all been holographic clones of each other, for all the difference between them.

Torres scowled at her slop as though contemplating being sick over it. "Does he provide your meals, too?"

Despite the edge in Torres's voice, the Ocampa

doctor smiled while he led them off the plaza toward a sea of neat, gray tables. "In fact, he does. He designed and built this entire city for us after the Warming. The food processors dispense nutritional supplements every four-point-one intervals." He looked at his own plate with a wistful tip of his head. "It may not offer the exotic tastes some of our young people crave these days, but it meets our needs."

Whether that said more about the Ocampa's needs, or about their Caretaker's sensitivity to them, Kim didn't care to speculate.

A monitor as long and tall as *Voyager*'s main viewscreen hung above the sprawl of tables, sprinkling the subterranean darkness with gentle images from a world these people could never have known from the insides of this huge stone tomb. Oceans and rivers flowed in idyllic splendor beneath a ripple of soothing music; forests and prairies melted softly over the watery images, until some small foraging rodent dominated the screen as it dug through a carpet of autumn leaves. All around the eating zone, placid Ocampa studied the ever-changing pictures with almost hypnotic intensity.

Kim nodded at the screen as he slid into a seat the doctor offered. "Is this how the Caretaker communicates with you?"

Glancing in the direction of Kim's nod, the doctor shook his head and sat as well. "He never communicates directly. We try to interpret his wishes as best we can."

"I'm curious . . ." Kim forced his eyes away from the weirdly captivating images, only to find himself drawn to a bank of similar screens on the opposite end of the alcove. He made himself focus on the Ocampa doctor instead. Torres remained stubbornly fixated on her food. "I'm curious to know how you've interpreted the Caretaker's reason for sending us here."

The doctor twirled what looked like a fork in the midst of his mash in an oddly human gesture of introspection. "We believe he must have separated you from your own species for their protection."

Torres slammed her utensils to the table with a crash. "Their *protection?*"

"From your illness." The doctor glanced uncertainly between them as Kim reached across to close his hand around her wrist. "Perhaps he is trying to prevent a plague."

"We weren't sick until we met your Caretaker," Torres pointed out.

Kim squeezed her wrist—hard—and earned a vicious glare from Torres right before she twisted effortlessly out of his grip and crushed his own hand in her fist. Refusing to give her the satisfaction of seeing him in pain, he ignored the discomfort as best he could and asked the doctor, "Why would he send us to you if he thought this is an infectious disease?"

"He must know we're immune. From time to time, he asks us to care for people with this disease. It's the least we can do to repay his—"

Torres released her hold on Kim to lunge across the table toward the doctor. "There have been *others* like us?"

The doctor jerked back in his seat, blinking in surprise. "Yes . . ."

"Where are they?"

He straightened carefully, and looked Torres firmly in the eye as he pushed the remnants of his meal to one side. "Your condition is very serious," he explained, carefully, as though thinking hard before he chose each word. "We don't know exactly how to treat it." He looked from Torres to Kim with a certain grim steadiness. "I'm afraid the others did not recover."

CHAPTER
13

TUVOK REALIZED HE SHOULD HAVE ANTICIPATED PROBlems when Neelix's warbled "Come in!" answered his signal at a volume below what human ears could have heard. Removed by several rooms, he instantly deduced from the slight Doppler shift and loss of harmonic complexity. And distracted by some other attention-intensive activity. Tuvok determined that he lacked sufficient data to speculate as to the nature of that activity, so let himself into Neelix's quarters as requested under the assumption that Neelix was not averse to interruptions.

The inside of the cabin smelled like a charnel house.

A moment's inspection revealed a majority of the stench emanating from the charred remains of some unfortunate creature, whose partially deconstructed skeleton had been displaced across the table, the bedding, the floor. Aware that his distaste for meat was a cultural and species-related bias, Tuvok carefully relocated the associated negative connotations to a portion of his brain that would not interfere with his ability to deal civilly with their visitor. His equally strong preferences for hygiene were not so easily subverted, however. Picking his way primly between piles of clothing, scatters of half-eaten fruit, and pitcher after pitcher of water, Tuvok had nearly dissociated from his physical self by the time he reached the bathroom door.

What he had taken at first for the squealing of heat-stressed water pipes was now more clearly discernible as some primitive musical construction. Tuvok thought it not unlike the wails Xerxes howler bats used to stun the lyre birds that were their primary prey. It seemed unlikely that Neelix had managed—or desired—to smuggle a howler bat onto the ship so far away from Federated space, but a renewed whooping from inside the roiling cloud of steam made it impossible for Tuvok to completely discount this hypothesis.

Pausing on the bathroom threshold, Tuvok spent only 7.05 seconds attempting to see past the wall of steam. Then, when it occurred to him that perhaps he wasn't truly interested in observing whatever went on inside it, he summoned simply, "Sir?," and waited for Neelix to disengage himself from whatever communion he and the howler bat were sharing.

Liquid splashed an instant's clarity through the steam as Neelix surged to the surface in a tub already overfilled with what appeared to be scalding hot water. "Mr. Vulcan! Come in, come in!" He smiled broadly, leaping sloppily to his feet to wave Tuvok forward with both arms.

In that instant, Tuvok learned more about the anatomy of Neelix's species than he had ever wanted to know.

"Please—I can hardly see you!"

How unfortunate that the limitation didn't go both ways.

Lifting his eyes to a point in the steam cloud several centimeters above Neelix's spotted head, Tuvok took a single precise step farther into the bathroom and folded his hands behind his back.

That little bit of capitulation was apparently enough. "I want to thank you for your hospitality," the lumpy little alien enthused. "I must admit, I haven't had access to a . . . a food replor—*replicator* before."

Tuvok raised an eyebrow. "I would never have guessed."

"And to immerse yourself in water!" He flopped back into his tub with a great splash. Tuvok horrified himself by flinching, however imperceptibly, when a spray of hot wetness lashed across the front of his uniform. "Do you know what a joy this is?"

The question seemed rhetorical, and Tuvok, engrossed in maintaining at least an appearance of dignity, was satisfied to let it lie unanswered.

"Nobody around here wastes water in this manner," Neelix went on, oblivious of his audience's suffering. "A good sand scrub—that's the best we can hope for." He twisted around to drag yet another pitcher from the shelf behind him, and poured the entire contents over his head with a delicious shiver.

Tuvok blinked his attention back to the nowhere spot in front of him. "I am pleased you are enjoying yourself," he said, "but we are in orbit of the fifth planet. We need your assistance."

Springing to his feet again, Neelix swiped water from himself almost gleefully, spraying wetness everywhere. "Could you hand me the towel?"

Cognizant of a length of terry cloth on the very edge of his peripheral vision, Tuvok snatched the towel from its rack without turning to look, and passed it equally blindly to the naked alien.

Neelix snapped it playfully at the Vulcan, then wilted just a little under the force of Tuvok's cold stare. Tuvok considered preparing a report for the little alien regarding Vulcan philosophy and psychology, with special emphasis on the fact that Vulcans had no sense of humor, nor did they want one. Or perhaps a steady program of negative reinforcement would be more effective—Neelix was already busily toweling himself dry, as though never having tested the limits of Vulcan endurance.

"If you will scan the southern continent," he said

as he stepped clear of the tub, "you'll find a range of extinct volcanoes. Follow the foothills north until you discover a dry riverbed." He made a sling with the towel to polish his ample backside. "You'll find an encampment there."

Tuvok committed the simple instructions to memory. "Do you believe our people might be at this location?"

"It's not impossible." Neelix shrugged and tossed the towel aside. "Maybe. Perhaps not." He smiled up at Tuvok as he pushed through the doorway in front of the Vulcan on his way to the main living chamber. "But we'll find them. We'll need several containers of water to bring for barter." He picked up a mostly fleshed bone at random as he wandered over to the control bank on the opposite wall. "Do these replicators make clothing, as well?"

Hoping to encourage that line of thought, Tuvok said only, "Yes."

"Will it make me a uniform like yours?"

The thought alone nearly broke through Tuvok's Vulcan control. "No," he made himself say, very clearly. "It most certainly will not."

Neelix gave a little grunt and turned back to the replicator with the half-gnawed bone sticking out of his mouth. Tuvok directed his attention toward the empty bathroom, studying the fractal patterns made by the puddles until Neelix indicated that it was safe to turn around.

* * *

Janeway took in as many details of the place as she could in the instant between first return of vision and the transporter effect's release. It didn't take long to absorb what little the landscape had to offer.

Sand. Sand, and more sand. Water had been gone so long from this land that the very skin of the ground had cracked and shrunken, leaving a scaly surface that looked like widely spaced stepping-stones with black fingers of nothing between them. Kilometers away to left and right, where the banks of this onetime river rose up to make ancient floodplains, broken structures with the height and regularity of artificial constructs sketched out a depressing hint of cities long gone. Of lives swallowed up by the dryness until only dust remained to chew away at the foundations and drag civilization's litter back down into the dirt from which it came.

In its place, a rude tent camp had sprung up in the middle of the hard-baked waterway. Spare, sun-darkened people froze and looked up at the transporter's whine. Their clothes were sand-blasted to the same dark tatter, their skin and eyes so burned by heat that it was hard to imagine any expressions but anger and hatred on their lean, wasted faces. Janeway took in the row of out-of-atmosphere ships lined up several hundred meters beyond the last building in the camp, and matched that strange incongruity to the obvious weapons slung across the backs of half the skinny desert people, and she made a note to herself not to underestimate these pitiful creatures. They hadn't managed to survive in such harsh conditions without knowing how to fight.

"Why would anyone want to live in a place like this?" Paris remarked with an inappropriate amount of disgust as soon as the transporter released them. He kicked up a cloud of powder-fine sand while Janeway watched the dirty aliens at the fringe of the camp boil into activity like a nest of disturbed ants. She wondered if it was their arrival or the deep thrumming she could feel through her feet that had the natives so excited.

Neelix moved up alongside her, following her gaze as he answered Paris. "The rich cormaline deposits are very much in demand."

"The Ocampa use it for barter?" Chakotay asked.

"Not the Ocampa." Neelix seemed vaguely irritated at the stupidity of the suggestion. "The Kazon-Ogla."

"Kazon-Ogla?" Janeway glanced down at him, and caught a flash of light from the corner of her eye. The pulses from the Array, she realized as she raised her head. They barely stood out in the full glare of the local sun, but she could just make out where they pounded the earth near the horizon, in time with the trembling at her feet. "Who are the Kazon-Ogla?"

Neelix waved down the dry riverbed toward the camp. "They are." He started forward without waiting for them, rubbing his hands with excitement. "Kazon sect controls this part of the quadrant. Some have water, some have ore, some have food. They all trade, and they all try to kill each other."

They sounded like a lovely people. Janeway motioned everyone to follow on Neelix's heels as more and more Kazon spilled out into the sun, their weapons drawn. "I thought you said the Ocampa had our people."

He waved off her question with brusque impatience, and Janeway exchanged a questioning look with Tuvok as the little alien scurried forward to meet the oncoming crowd of growling Kazon. "My friends! It's good to see you again!" The Vulcan studiously gave no hint as to what he thought of Neelix's peremptory behavior, but Janeway hadn't been his commander so long for nothing. In whatever arcane way Vulcan body language seemed to work, she'd already gotten the distinct impression that Tuvok didn't care for Neelix overmuch.

Apparently, his dislike of the little alien wasn't so uncommon a thing. Kazon surged around him with an angry roar, hefting him into the air above their heads and shaking him the way a dog shakes a well-mangled toy as they chanted and shouted and danced back toward the village. Janeway put out a hand to stop Paris from drawing his phaser as even more of the natives swept into a ring around the landing party. *In another few minutes,* she promised him silently, *our Universal Translators should kick in. Then we can talk to them.* In the meantime, they had the option of beaming out no matter how many Kazon surrounded them, and there was no way the Kazon could suspect that. Janeway had no intention of starting a war with these people if she could avoid it—not while they might be the only link to finding Kim and Torres. Holding her arms wide to let the Kazon disarm her without a fight, Janeway kept a steady eye on Paris and Chakotay to make sure they did the same, however grudgingly. *A few more minutes . . .*

"Wait! Wait!" Neelix's cry sounded like a pig's squealing, although Janeway suspected he was trying for an undertone of friendly laughter. "Yes, it's always wonderful to be back with you," he enthused as the mob carried him roughly into the outskirts of camp, "but I must speak with your Maje, the ever-wise Jabin—!"

One of the Kazon women—a whipcord demon with eyes as black as jet—yanked Neelix by the collar until he fell with a grunt at the base of a crumbling wall, where she could yell at him unobstructed by the others. "Very amusing," he coughed, scrabbling to his knees. "Very amusing—I enjoy a joke as much as the next man—" He looked up into the line of primitive rifles directed at his face, and an unexpected spasm of happiness flashed across his features. "Jabin! My old friend!"

Janeway turned in unison with the rest of the Kazon, leaving only the black-eyed female to rant at Neelix and slap at his head. Near the back of the crowd, a tall, big-handed man as dark and cracked as the dirt pushed his way forward. From the hateful glimmer in his eyes, he would have bitten Neelix in half with his own teeth as soon as look at him. Snapping an order to the impromptu firing squad, he smiled thinly across their heads at Neelix and lifted his arm in the universal signal.

"Water!" Neelix blurted, his voice squeezed into a frightened squeak. "I have water to replace all that I borrowed!"

The Kazon froze, eyes eager at the prospect of slaking their thirst, and looked back toward Jabin. Their leader stood equally unmoving, but Janeway could see the storms of thought raging just behind his eyes.

Sensing a chance for reprieve, Neelix pointed a trembling finger at Janeway. "Their ship has technology that can make water out of thin air!" Which was better than trying to explain the transporter, so Janeway let him have that slight untruth.

Jabin shoved aside two of his people to stalk closer to the captive landing party. He looked like a stick, almost thin enough to snap, and smelled like rotten sweat and salty oil. Janeway found herself hoping fervently that Kim and Torres hadn't been locked up with these people—she'd almost rather they were dead.

Without being told, Paris unhooked his canteen

and tossed it to Jabin. Jabin did no more than sniff it before letting the others tear it away.

Janeway never saw a drop of the water escape anyone's lips. They sucked straight from the mouth of the can, or from each other, scrabbling and shouting like dogs over a bone. Now Jabin met Janeway's eyes steadily and pointed at the canteen hanging from her own belt. "You have more?"

More than the few mouthfuls any of us happen to carry. Enough to start a full-scale riot, in fact, from the look of things. Tapping her comm badge, she hoped they had guessed rightly about how to present themselves to these Kazon. "Janeway to *Voyager.* Energize."

The vats sparkled into existence back where the landing party had first set down. Startlingly, she could smell the cool freshness of water on the parched air, and the crowd surrounding them gave a cry of desperate hope. They broke apart into a stream of individuals, flowing around and away from Janeway's people with a readiness that lifted the tension from her heart. Splashes and glad ululations drew even more natives out of their huts, and Janeway watched them converge on their simple abundance for a moment before turning back to Jabin. "There's more where that came from, if you can help us."

He pulled his eyes away from the sight of so much water with obvious effort. Anger and fear mixed on his face in that peculiar combination Janeway had learned to recognize in men who fear for their status when confronted with a threat they suspect is their better. "How can we help someone so powerful they can create water out of thin air?"

Maybe Neelix's lie hadn't been so harmless after all. "This man—" She pointed to where Neelix now huddled fearfully close to Tuvok's elbow. "—led us here suggesting we might find a people called the Ocampa. Do you know where they are?"

Jabin made a face, as though she'd asked him to chew his own feces. "Ocampa?" Turning, he jerked his chin back toward the sorry hovels, where a small crowd of young and injured Kazon were making their slower way forward. "She is Ocampa." And Janeway's eyes caught on a single pale, ghostly figure standing at the back of the gathering.

The girl was fragile and small, and her sun-spun hair still floated in the dry air despite the dirt streaking it with brassy gold. Her eyes were large, her skin as smooth and fine as eggshell, but the angry welts of color on her face and arms weren't all from sunburn. Janeway felt a fist of anger push against her chest, and fought it down with effort. But she prayed all over again that Kim and Torres hadn't been found by these creatures who thought so little of savaging such a thing of innocent beauty.

As if to secure her poor opinion of his band, Jabin spat in the Ocampa's general direction and waved at her as though to banish her from his sight. "Why would you be interested in these worthless creatures? They only live nine years. And they make poor servants. We caught this one when she wandered to the surface."

"The surface?" Janeway glanced away from the Ocampa girl—who, despite Jabin's dismissal, crept silently closer as the Kazon pack moved, her eyes playing across the landing party as though expecting them to transform into something more recognizable. "You mean they live underground."

Jabin grunted and shook a fist at the white fire scarring the sky as the Array's pulses burned past. "The entity in space that gives them food and power also gave them sole access to the only *water* on this world." He spat again (dryly, Janeway noted, with only the explosive burst of air through his lips to express his disdain). "Two miles below the surface."

It seemed the Array hadn't made many friends at all in this section of space. "This same entity has abducted two of our people," Janeway told him. He squinted at her with interest, but didn't interrupt. "We believe they might be with the Ocampa."

Jabin shrugged. "There's no way to get to them. We've tried." As though forcible attack were the only way any sane being would approach the problem. "The entity has established some kind of subterranean barrier we cannot penetrate."

"But *she* got out." Chakotay gestured at the girl, who now stood close enough for them to see the color of her bright eyes, but still outside Jabin's easy reach.

The Kazon leader shot a glare at her, and the

Ocampa moved a few more steps away from him, circling to stand on a line with Tuvok and Neelix. "Occasionally," the Kazon grumbled, "some do find their way to the surface. We don't know how. But the Ocampa always seal the tunnels afterward."

Neelix spared a stiff smile for the silent girl. "Maybe she could help these good people find a way down."

"You'd be wasting your time with her," Jabin told him. "I've used every method of persuasion I know to get her to help *us.*" He scowled at her darkly. "She won't."

Neelix transferred his smile just as readily to the Kazon. "Then she's worthless to you. Let us trade you water for the scrawny little thing." He waved his fingers at the girl, as though she were too distasteful to consider touching.

Jabin peered from Neelix to the Ocampa, and Janeway got the impression he was trying to decide which one he hated more. "I would be more interested in acquiring this—" Suddenly, his keen eyes locked on Janeway, and he smiled coldly. "—technology that allows you to create water."

Janeway shook her head. "That would be difficult. It's integrated into our ship's systems." She was definitely never, ever going to let Neelix establish the grounds from which they negotiated again.

Jabin barked a command to a handful of the Kazon who still immersed their arms in the now half-empty water vats, sucking down great handfuls between their laughter and coarse comments. They broke away instantly at his call, and Jabin drew them into a huddle around him so they could growl back and forth among themselves without Janeway's people hearing. Janeway drummed her fingers impatiently against one leg. He wasn't a stupid man, this Jabin. His danger lay in the fact that he still wasn't as smart as he believed himself to be.

A warm, certain thought sprang to the forefront of Janeway's brain without warning. *Do not trust them. They will never let me go.* She blinked, startled, and glanced at Paris and Chakotay for some sign that they had heard it, too. She found the Indian staring in amazement at the girl, while the Ocampa looked back with frank intensity, not at all intimidated by his attention.

Jabin broke apart his impromptu council with a wave of his arms. "I have decided to keep the Ocampa female," he announced loudly. Two of his companions brought their weapons to bear on Janeway, and the Kazon leader followed up with a greasy smile. *"And* all of you."

It wasn't as if Janeway hadn't expected some sort of treachery from this Kazon Maje. It just irritated her when small-minded dictators started acting like they could push everyone else around as easily as they did their terrorized subjects. She sighed and crossed her arms.

"Tell them to drop their weapons!"

Janeway would never have guessed Neelix could move so fast. One instant, he was glued to Tuvok's side, his eyes on the lovely Ocampa girl—the next, he was practically clinging to the front of Jabin's tunic, a small hand weapon that Janeway hadn't even known he'd carried shoved under the Maje's chin. She didn't know whether to be amused at his audacity, or alarmed at his capacity for deceit.

"Drop them, my friends," Neelix commanded again, looking around meaningfully at the Kazon who still brandished weapons. "Or he dies in an instant."

The pure loathing pouring from Jabin's face could have fused neutronium. Still, he jerked a stiff wave at his followers, and one by one the rifles lowered. Janeway waited until the last of them had clattered to the ground before signaling Tuvok and Paris to retrieve their phasers and whatever other equipment the Kazon had taken.

Neelix darted a nervous look back toward Janeway, chewing his lower lip. "Come on!" She scowled at him, not appreciating his attempts to hurry her, then bit off whatever she might have said when the Ocampa girl broke away from the Kazon crowd to clasp Neelix's open hand.

He pushed Jabin back with as much roughness as his little body could muster, then dragged the Ocampa with him as he hurried to cluster with Janeway. "I strongly suggest you get us out of here!" he gasped as he ducked in behind her.

She decided to twist the details of his reasoning out of him later. She slapped at her comm badge. "Six to beam up!"

The transporter beam whisked away the desert bleakness before Jabin had even clambered to his knees.

Voyager's clean gray walls rippled into being around them on the scent of fresh, humidified air. Janeway had never realized how much she had taken such a simple thing as moisture for granted. Turning, she fixed Neelix with a stern glower, prepared to tell him—she didn't know what. All semblance of anger bled from her mind the moment she saw Neelix wrapped around the slim Ocampa, her face buried against the side of his neck as she clutched herself against him.

"My dearest!" Neelix sighed, pulling back to gaze at her in naked adoration. "Didn't I promise I'd save you?"

CHAPTER
14

KIM SAT WITH HIS HEAD IN HIS HAND AND WATCHED
Torres pace from one end of the stark courtyard to
the other, too tired to join her, much less put effort
into making her sit down. She'd been roaming
between the food dispensers and anemic sculptures
ever since the Ocampa doctor left them with the
remains of their half-eaten lunches. Looking for a
way out, Kim assumed. Still, she hadn't strayed
beyond even the closest walkway so far, and if her
quick, angry mind was busy working on some sort
of elaborate escape plan, she hadn't bothered to
share it with Kim.

Maybe, like him, there was part of her that
realized that searching an underground metropolis
for something the natives said didn't even exist

probably required a fairly massive time commitment. And, at the moment, Kim wasn't confident that either of them should be making long-term plans. He didn't think he'd be able to walk from the eating courtyard to his bed in the infirmary, much less hike all the way to the distant surface. *I'll feel better in a little while,* he told himself as Torres stalked past again. *I'll sit here until my stomach settles, then we'll figure out how to get back to the others.* He was really sorry he'd eaten everything the doctor had insisted on earlier, though.

He followed Torres's progress with his eyes, not lifting his chin from his hand. "I'm sure Captain Janeway is doing everything she can to find us," he offered the next time the Maquis passed within earshot.

Torres made a noise that fell somewhere between a laugh and a sigh. "What makes you think any of them are still alive?"

Because the prospects otherwise were too frightening to consider just now. Because if he allowed himself to believe that everything and everyone he knew on this side of the galaxy were gone, then he'd have to admit that his chances of ever seeing home again had vanished with them. Because he didn't think he could make himself escape if there was nothing left worth escaping for.

He didn't know how to tell Torres all that without somehow making it all real.

Torres paused at the edge of the plaza, her back to him, and Kim thought for a moment that she was contemplating another frantic bolt. Then she swayed sickly and made a blind grab for one of the tables as her knees began to go. Kim lunged from his seat without thinking. He reached her only an instant ahead of his own nausea. "Should I call for some help?" he asked, clinging to her and half-hoping she'd say yes.

Instead: "No!" Torres clung to his arm in turn with fingers that Kim knew would leave bruises for weeks—assuming they both lived that long.

"Are you in pain?" another voice asked worriedly from behind them.

If Kim hadn't expected Torres to whirl the instant he heard the stranger's voice, the Maquis's violent reaction might have knocked him to the ground. As it was, they collided as they both turned, and Kim ended up mostly in front, his arm thrown out to herd Torres behind him—more for fear of what she might do to their unexpected visitor than because he harbored any illusions about protecting her.

"Are you watching us?" Torres pushed against him from behind, but made no real effort to muscle past him. The Ocampa woman who'd startled them recoiled a step all the same, as though sensing how much trouble the bigger Maquis could cause. "I thought we weren't supposed to be your prisoners."

Kim saw the Ocampa blink and shake her head slowly, and realized that she didn't have to imagine how Torres could be if she went out of control. This was the same nurse who had smiled down at Kim on that first morning—the one who'd watched Torres nearly tear apart every attendant in the infirmary on her way toward the door. She knew exactly what she was dealing with.

"I wasn't watching you," the nurse said softly, taking a step onto the plaza. "I was coming to give you something." She glanced nervously left and right, then minced the rest of the way toward them as though speed would somehow hide her actions. Caught by the earnest anxiety on her waiflike features, Kim came forward to meet her halfway. She took his hand and pressed a small green vial into his palm. "I don't know if it'll help," she admitted in a near whisper. "It's a medicine." She glanced over Kim's head with an uncertain smile as Torres moved up to join them. "There are people who have broken from tradition and left the city. Their colony grows fruit and vegetables. They discovered quite by accident that the moss that grows on certain fruit trees has healing properties." She touched the vial with one finger, and a fearful unease settled over her face again. "I'm . . . sorry for what's happened to you."

It was the first time any of the Ocampa had indicated that this illness, these growths, had somehow been *done* to them, and weren't just something they'd arrived already carrying. Kim was intrigued by the significance of this changed attitude.

"We appreciate this," he told her, closing his

fingers gratefully around the vial. "But the only way we're going to survive is if we can get to the surface and find our people."

An expression that was almost bitterness pressed the nurse's mouth into a line. "The elders would say that's against the Caretaker's wishes."

"What do *you* say?" Torres pressed. Her voice was challenging, but surprisingly gentle.

The nurse looked abruptly away, and Kim saw her easy skepticism of a moment before give way all too quickly to childlike confusion. "The Caretaker . . ." She shook her head slowly, biting her lower lip. "The Caretaker has been behaving strangely for the past several months . . ." She shrugged uncertainly. ". . . abducting people, increasing the power supply . . ."

Kim exchanged a glance with Torres. "Power supply?" he asked the nurse.

The Ocampa looked at him as though surprised he had to ask. "He's tripled the energy he sends us. They say we have enough stored now to run the city for five years."

The thought reminded Kim too much of the Armageddon hideaways from the crazy days at the end of the twentieth century. It wasn't a pleasant image. "Nobody knows why?"

"When we ask, we're told to trust the Caretaker's decisions." She fell silent suddenly, turning away with her hands folded thoughtfully beneath her chin.

Silence, Kim's mother was fond of saying, was

persuasion's greatest ally. What crying, ranting, and threats might fail to accomplish, a few well-placed minutes of silence could usually bring about. Over the years, Kim had seen the power of silence win his mother a registered Pekingese, secure his father's permission for Kim to attend Youth Orchestra summer camp, and convince an entire crowd of rowdy teenagers that they didn't really want to shout obscenities at passing drivers. Kim couldn't wield silence with quite the mastery his mother displayed, but he practiced it from time to time, and had faith he'd someday get better. "Remember," his mother had told him. "If you stay silent long enough, people will talk themselves into doing what they already know is right. There's nothing you could say or do that would possibly work any better than they will on themselves."

So, with those words ringing in his memory—words spoken by a voice his heart now despaired of ever hearing again—Kim waited in dutiful silence while the nurse paced four steps away from them, then turned and slowly made her way back.

"One person I knew," she said carefully, *"did* get to the surface. We never saw her again."

Kim felt Torres's hand clamp hard on his shoulder. "How?" he asked the nurse.

She looked up with a certain tense bravery. "The ancient tunnels that brought us here still exist. Over the years, small breaches in the security barrier have appeared, just large enough for someone to get through. But it still requires digging through meters of rock to get out," she added quickly, her eyes flicking up to Torres as though reacting to something in the Maquis's face.

"Can you get us tools to dig with?" Torres asked, undeterred.

The nurse was already shaking her head. "It would take days, maybe even weeks, to break through. You have to rest—conserve your strength."

"Please . . ." Kim squeezed her hand, and tried to let her see the very real pain and urgency that had been gnawing at him ever since waking up so far away from his people. "It's our only chance."

The nurse stared down at their entwined hands, and Kim gave her as long as she needed for silence to do its work. When she finally sighed and looked up in frustrated reluctance, Kim knew the battle was won. Still, he only nodded mute thanks, and let the silence say whatever else was needed.

Janeway had never met the emergency medical program before. She wasn't sure she had met it now. Flashing from place to place in the still half-damaged sickbay, it concentrated on its alien patient with a single-mindedness that Janeway suspected few flesh-and-blood doctors could rival. Given the amount of heated discussion boiling among the half-dozen people crammed into the little space, she envied the computer its concentration. Still, it would have been nice to see it smile, or interact with the delicate Ocampa in some manner other than a strictly mechanical one. *When we get home,* she promised the snippily busy program, *I'm going to talk to somebody about installing some bedside manner into your next upgrade.* Although she wondered if such a thing really mattered when the program only hung around for an hour or so, pending the arrival of new medical personnel. Probably not enough to justify the cost of retooling the whole program. Which, she thought as she watched the hologram manipulate the Ocampa's arm into a new position with businesslike abruptness, was really too bad.

The girl's name was Kes, and what she saw in Neelix was a mystery to Janeway. On the other hand, what Neelix saw in Kes wasn't at all hard to figure out. She was tiny and slight, with eyes as blue as colored glass and as big as a full moon. A simple, angelic beauty cloaked her like a silken robe, and the sheer innocence of her smile lent it a brilliance even Janeway found hard to ignore. Neelix hadn't released her hand since the planet's surface, and Janeway didn't think Paris had remembered to blink since right around the same time. Even Chakotay seemed embarrassed every time he found himself staring—which was apparently more often than he would have liked, judging from the recurrent darkening of his high-boned cheeks. Only Tuvok and the medical program seemed completely unaffected by Kes's beauty, and Janeway wasn't placing any bets on what kind of thoughts really went on beneath the surface of Tuvok's Vulcan calm.

For now, though, the security chief seemed more concerned with the etiquette of Kes's rescue than with the girl herself. "If you had told us what you had planned," he was explaining for perhaps the fifth time to Neelix, "we might have anticipated your irrational behavior—"

"Irrational?" Neelix sniffed with an indignation that didn't suit his cuddly appearance. "We got out of there, didn't we?"

The Vulcan lifted one eyebrow as though inclined to comment, but the Ocampa girl interrupted before he could actually speak. "Excuse me . . ."

Every male in the place—Tuvok included—fixated on her with stunning suddenness. So much for Vulcan control. Janeway smothered a smile behind one hand.

"Don't blame Neelix," Kes pleaded, stroking the alien's head almost absently. "It's all my fault. I—"

"That's enough." The hologram stepped back from her to angle a stern glare at the rest of the room. "This is a sickbay, not a conference room." It locked a particularly irate scowl on Janeway. "Visiting hours are over. Everyone except my patient is to leave immediately—"

"Computer." Janeway never broke the hologram's gaze. "End medical holographic program."

The doctor got as far as opening its mouth to

protest before blinking out of existence. Janeway stepped away from the wall to retrieve the medical scanner the hologram had dropped upon its exit, and nodded that Kes should continue as she came across to stand beside her bed.

The girl offered Janeway the same lovely smile as she'd given the men. *You just don't know what you have over them, do you?* Janeway wasn't sure whether to laugh or sigh.

"I never should have gone to the surface," Kes said, looking among all the faces standing around her. "I'm too curious. I'm told it's my worst failing—"

"No, no," Neelix cooed against her hand. "It's a *wonderful* quality, your most endearing."

Kes looked down at him in obvious appreciation of his kindness. "But it does get me in trouble. I knew the Kazon might find me—"

"Those brutes—kidnapping you!"

Janeway waved Neelix into silence, then felt immediately guilty when he stared at her in amazement, as though completely unaware that he'd been gushing out loud.

"But if they hadn't," Kes went on, "I'd never have met you." Still smiling lovingly at Neelix, she explained to Janeway, "Neelix stole water from the Kazon and gave it to me."

Which, given the situation on the surface, was no doubt the greatest act of love anyone could ever hope for. "Is it possible our crew members are being held captive by your people?" Janeway asked.

She'd explained to Kes what they'd learned from Neelix and the Kazon on the way from the transporter room, but hadn't been able to get past Neelix's fretting enough to get much in the way of answers before now.

Kes tucked an errant strand of hair behind one ear, and frowned consideration. "We would never hold anyone captive. But the Caretaker has sent aliens to us who are sick and need care."

"Sick?" Chakotay came a few steps closer, open concern on his face. "What's wrong with them?

"I'm not sure." Kes shrugged; then her face melted into an expression as purely sad as her contrition had been sincere. "But none of them has ever survived."

Never a good sign, that. Janeway thought again about Kim's mother, waiting patiently for her only son to return, and she had to force the image angrily out of her head. "Would you be willing to take us underground to look for our missing crew?" she asked.

Kes shook her head sadly. "Jabin was right." She sounded like she was apologizing for the fact. "There's no way to get down. The tunnel I came out has been sealed."

It seemed a ridiculously small obstacle, considering everything else that had happened of late. "We don't need a tunnel," the captain explained. "We have the ability to transport there directly."

"Captain . . ." Tuvok turned his attention pointedly away from the girl when Janeway looked to him. "Our sensors did not pick up any indication of an underground civilization. The subterranean barrier Jabin described may be responsible. It might also block our transporter."

Janeway cursed quietly. Why could nothing be as simple as it sounded? *I'm not asking for the world here! Just the life of one boy on my crew.* It made her long for the days when you could force cooperation out of the gods through something as straightforward as physical combat.

"There are breaches in the security barrier," Kes offered eagerly, "where it's begun to decay. That's how I got out."

A start, at least. "Have the transporter room begin a sweep for any breaches we might be able to beam through," Janeway told Tuvok.

The Vulcan nodded, heading for the door, and Janeway turned back to their visitors to find Neelix blinking after the security chief as though worried about what Tuvok had gone to do. He caught Janeway looking at him, and jumped slightly, his face growing dark with embarrassment.

"Kes can tell you where to go," Neelix said—but carefully, his hands still firmly clasping both of Kes's. "But now that she's free, we're leaving this system together."

Kes looked down at him, obviously surprised. "These people rescued me."

Neelix pouted up at her. *"I* rescued you," he protested, and Kes made a disapproving face.

"With their help. It would be wrong not to help them now."

Janeway couldn't help but wonder what sort of thoughts went through Neelix that made him deflate so at Kes's disagreement, only to swell with love and wonder an instant later when he looked up into the Ocampa's eyes. "Isn't she remarkable?" he said with a sigh, to no one in particular.

Janeway shook her head, struck again by the easy willingness with which men let themselves be enslaved, only to smile privately to herself when Paris answered Neelix dreamily, "Yes . . . She is."

CHAPTER

15

JANEWAY SENSED THE WEIGHT OF ROCK ABOVE HER THE instant the transporter beam released them. Not claustrophobia—tight spaces and enclosed rooms were her venue and lifeblood on board starships— but, rather, a maddeningly acute awareness of the meters and tons of living planet that hovered above her like a precariously balanced sword of Damocles.

She'd discovered this sensation the first time she let Mark talk her into an overnight caving expedition. He said it would be fun. While he slept blissfully through a night of whatever underground wonders so entranced him, Janeway lay through that eight-hour stretch of total darkness with the ominous pressure of a ten-meter-thick ceiling only a handspan above her face, keeping her awake and adrenaline-powered until their subterranean guide reinstated the lights and announced it was time to move on. Mark accused her later of being scared of the dark; she hadn't been able to convince him that it wasn't the dark that made her uncomfortable, but the huge, capricious geology that held the dark inside. Just because it had chosen to hold its shape for something like three and a half million years seemed little reason to believe it would continue to do so over the next three hours.

They never went caving again.

Now that same feeling came rushing back on her, although nowhere near as strongly as before. Having a ceiling so tall it almost masqueraded for sky helped, as did the gentle, indirect lighting that seemed to cast delicate shadows in all directions. Still, not even the absence of walls in the immediate vicinity or the dramatic view of a distant city against the glowering horizon could completely distract her from the lack of a true sun blazing overhead, or the lank, clammy stillness of the air. A cave, by any other name.

A small group of Ocampa looked up as the transporter's chime died away, looking interested but hardly terrified at the prospect of strangers appearing out of nowhere into their sheltered world. Short rows of anemic plants climbed trellises strung between banks of flowstone, while brilliant white lights had been erected every dozen meters or so to substitute for the reality of a native star. Janeway wondered how the people patiently hauling water to each of the tiny rows had managed to hack out of the growing troughs, much less find the dirt to fill them, and wondered, too, if the presence of the green growing things made any real difference to the starkness of their cave-born lives.

"Captain . . ." Tuvok moved alongside her, his tricorder aimed upward and singing faintly. "The pulses from the Array continue to accelerate. The intervals between them have decreased another point-eight seconds."

And was that good or bad? Janeway tried to listen for the deep thrum of the energy beam's arrival through the muffling layers of stone, and wasn't sure if what she heard was the Array's pounding or her own heartbeat in her ears.

"Kes!"

One of the farmers recognized the girl still clinging to Neelix's hand, and suddenly a burble of excitement swept through the other workers at the sound of Kes's name. They each took a moment to carefully set aside their crocks and tools, then descended on the landing party with cries of delight that sounded like children heading out for recess as much as anything else. They were all young and pleasantly thin, Janeway noticed as they gathered into a babbling knot around Kes to exchange hugs and brotherly kisses. It was like being surrounded by a crowd of half-finished adolescents who had only just started to be good at mimicking their parents' adulthood.

"Hello, Daggin." Kes smiled when the man who'd first called out to her swept her up in his arms. Neelix, on the other hand, looked considerably less pleased.

Still grinning, Daggin pushed Kes away from him to hold her at arm's length, shaking his head as though unable to believe she were real. "We never thought we'd see you again! How did you get back?"

"These people rescued me from the Kazon," Kes told him, flashing a shy smile up at Janeway. "I'm trying to help them find two of their crewmen." She turned in a half-circle to call to the other Ocampa around them, "Does anyone know where the aliens are kept? The ones the Caretaker sends here?"

Silence smothered the joyfulness of a moment before as swiftly as a hand over a candle flame. Janeway wondered if it was the mention of off-world aliens that made them so cautious, or the mention of their own Caretaker.

"I think they're at the central clinic," Daggin said after a moment.

Janeway touched Kes's shoulder with quiet hope. "Can you take us there?"

No. A new, deeper voice that was somehow both spoken and yet not quite heard seemed to come from nowhere. *She cannot.*

Kes had no difficulty turning to find the speaker behind the farmers to her right. Janeway was startled to see two Ocampa males as round and grounded as the others were fairylike and young. The older of the two, his pale, clear eyes squinted in a frown of unhappiness, pushed gently through the crowd to stand just in front of Kes as the girl explained, "They can't speak telepathically, Toscat. Please talk aloud."

The concept of Toscat—or anyone—slipping his words so casually inside her mind gave Janeway a chill. At least the Vulcans had the decency to ask permission before opening any sort of contact that might expose whatever random thoughts happened to occur to either party. Living in a race of telepaths must make keeping secrets a serious challenge. Janeway decided it might be best to keep Tuvok's inherited abilities to themselves, at least for the time being. No telling when the captain might decide they needed an informational edge, and Tuvok's willingness to attach himself to an Ocampa's thoughts would be worthless if the Ocampa already knew to protect themselves from the Federation visitors.

Toscat pursed his lips as though displeased with the idea of words passing through them, then nodded stiffly toward Janeway without actually meeting her eyes. "I didn't mean to be rude," he said, his voice too loud, and stilted with non-use. "But you should not be here."

"We'll be glad to leave," Janeway told him, "once we find our crewmen."

He looked up at her somewhat sharply then, and

Janeway met his gaze firmly. He wasn't the first person who'd tried to interfere with her duty to her crew, but he was hardly the most threatening. She held him pinned with her stare until he glanced aside again, ostensibly gathering Paris and Chakotay into the discussion although Janeway could plainly see the smears of red darkening on his translucent cheeks.

"That won't be possible," Toscat said, addressing the landing party as one large whole. "We cannot interfere with the Caretaker's wishes."

Chakotay snorted. "Maybe you can't, but we can."

The elder Ocampa shook his head. "You don't understand—"

"That's right." Kes touched Toscat's arm and made him look at her again. "They don't understand," she said, softly but with strength. "They have no way of knowing that the Ocampa have been dependent on the Caretaker for so long, we can't even *think* for ourselves anymore. They don't understand we were once a people who had full command of our minds' abilities—"

"The stories of our ancestors' cognitive abilities are apocryphal." Toscat aimed the explanation at Janeway, as though it were important that she understand. "At the very least, exaggerated."

"We *lost* those abilities," Kes said over him, more loudly, "because we stopped using them."

Toscat waved his hands in front of his face as though to banish her words from his sight. "We should not dwell on what's been lost, but on all that's been gained."

"Yes." Kes's voice dripped with a frustration that bordered dangerously on disdain. "We've gained a talent for dependence. For simply taking what we're given." She shook her head at Toscat, and took up Neelix's hand again in a gesture of clear defiance. "I'm going to help them whether you like it or not, Toscat. And I think my friends will join me."

The young farmers all around them murmured agreement, and Toscat flushed again as he shot a scowl into the quiet crowd. "You defied the Caretaker by going to the surface, Kes. Learn from the experience. Follow the path he has set for us."

Kes sniffed a little laugh. "I've learned very well, Toscat. *I saw the sunlight!*" Groans that could only have been from painful longing tore from half the assembled Ocampa. Janeway's heart went out to them, knowing—if only a little—what it must be like to grow up under the brow of the earth without even the touch of the sun. "I can't believe that our Caretaker would forbid us to open our eyes and see the sky," Kes went on. She looked proudly up at Janeway, then back at the other Federation men behind her. "Come on. We'll find your people."

She spun with rigid determination, Neelix scurrying along behind her in a daze of wide-eyed admiration. Janeway watched Toscat as the knot of farmers broke apart into a quiet stream to follow Kes down through the gardens, leaving the elder to wring his hands in the front of his robe and shake his head somewhat sadly. A parent, unhappy with the road his children have taken.

Confident that his disapproval might sink into despair but never over into violence, Janeway motioned her people to stay with her, and started after Kes toward the still far-distant city.

CHAPTER
16

THEY'D KNOWN THE TUNNELS WOULD BE LONG, AND dark, Kim reminded himself. The Ocampa nurse had warned them of that—more than once, even—before smuggling them out of the infirmary what felt like an eternity ago. Somehow, though, all her warnings had only made Kim more certain that he understood what to expect. They seemed to leave so little to his imagination. But now, aching in every muscle as though he'd been beaten, and barely able to force his body to take the next upward step, Kim wished he'd imagined more, and that he'd had the sense to believe in his imaginings.

For all her descriptions and cautions, the nurse still hadn't managed to capture the dank hopelessness of the place. The tunnels were barely high enough to stand upright in—some of them weren't. A rickety spiral of metal stairs climbed the sides of passages that faced straight upward, and the metal creaked and crackled with every bouncing step, as if gathering itself to plunge down into the darkness below. Wetness dripped, dropped from the rock all around them, and Kim thought he smelled the peculiar sweetness of rotten fabric more than once as they crawled or climbed through the dampness. He didn't try to hunt down the source of the stench.

Torres insisted that they use their flashlights as sparingly as possible, since neither they nor the Ocampa had the faintest idea how long the old devices would last. "If we keep going up," the Maquis had stated quite reasonably, "we'll know we're going in the right direction." That seemed a little simplistic to Kim, but it wasn't any worse an assumption than the one that said they'd be able to climb out in the first place, so he didn't question it. It was cold and lonely in the darkness, though. He wished the single-file construction of the tunnels didn't keep them too separated to at least hold hands.

Kim's foot banged against a webbed metal runner, and he stumbled to his knees with a crash that echoed through the chamber so loudly that it completely drowned out his accompanying cry of pain. *I don't want to do this,* a weak little voice inside him said. *I don't want to climb anymore. I don't want to hurt. I just want to go home and be done with all this*. Instead, he remained crouched over the heavy tool pack he'd dropped onto the stair above him, and waited for the pain and dizziness to go away.

Light exploded like a bombshell in his head, and Kim groaned as he buried his face harder against his hands. On the other end of the newly lit flashlight, Torres came back down a few clanging steps to stand above him. "Come on."

The pure whiteness of the artificial light felt like it was burning through the back of his skull. Kim only shook his head. He was ready to stay.

"Don't let it beat you, Starfleet." A startlingly gentle hand fitted itself under his elbow, encouraging him to stand without forcing him. "Come on," Torres said again, more plaintively.

He lifted his head and made himself sit back until he could look up into Torres's eyes. She'd moved the flashlight behind her, so that the light was more diffuse. It set her off from the darkness like a wild-maned troll. Kim wanted to stand for her, wanted to be strong and angry as she was, so that he could earn the right to live and see his family again. But everything looped and pitched too sickly, and he couldn't force his breathing to slow down and clear the pain out of his thinking. "I'm sorry," he muttered, sinking his head down into his hands again.

Torres's face creased with unaccustomed sensitivity, and she let go of his elbow as though afraid that moving too quickly would break him. "It's all right. We'll rest a minute." She sat without taking her eyes off him, crossing her hands over her knees.

Kim tried to smile up at her, but was afraid the expression came closer to fear than friendliness. "Maybe I'd do better if I had a little Klingon blood in me."

She made a gruff sound of amusement for his benefit. "Trust me. It's more trouble than it's worth."

As badly as he hurt now compared to her Amazonian composure, he had trouble believing that was true. Stiffening to will away another spasm of ghostly pain, he didn't even try to shrug off the hand she rested silently on his shoulder. He shook his head, choked with laughter at the irony of it all. "I spent my whole life getting ready for Starfleet. And on my very first mission . . ." He reached up blindly to twine his fingers with hers. ". . . I'm going to die. . . ."

Her hand closed tightly around his. "We're not finished yet. I know a few things old Sneezy didn't teach in his Survival Course."

The remark seemed to come out of nowhere. "Sneezy?"

"Commander Zakarian." Torres smiled at his confusion, and Kim thought he sensed a certain underlying relief in the way she playfully joggled his arm. "Remember? He must've been allergic to everything."

A sudden vivid memory of a lean, white-haired instructor with eyes as red as his face flashed across Kim's mind. They'd been in the Appalachians, and had been forced to cut the excursion short when something in the local flora shut down Zakarian's breathing without warning. Kim's Academy class had made an especially good grade for finding its way from wilderness to civilization without instructor guidance in record time. *"You* went to the Academy?"

"Actually made it into the second year before we 'mutually agreed' it wasn't the place for me." She smiled as though the memory didn't bother her, but Kim recognized Starfleet's euphemism for expulsion. He squeezed her hand in sympathy, and, just as quickly as it had come, the moment of rapport passed and she pulled her fingers from his grip. "I fit in a lot better with the Maquis," she finished with a shrug.

"You know," Kim told her, "I never really *liked* Zakarian." It was easier than what he would have liked to say.

Torres seemed to hear him both ways. Grinning somewhat wickedly, she chucked him under the chin, then pointedly settled back on her step to stare up in the direction they still had to go, giving Kim his minute to rest, but nothing more.

The sculptures in the open courtyard rattled, dancing about on their bases as the thundering shocks from the Array's pulsed signals grew in power and speed. Janeway looked up, peripherally aware of every other Ocampa in the vicinity echoing the gesture with a little cry of surprise. Unlike whatever the Ocampa were looking for, Janeway didn't really expect to see anything. When a sound as pervasive and intrusive as the hammering of these pulses rained down on you from overhead, though, there was just some human instinct that made you look up to see where the noise was coming from. As though by catching sight of the demon, that somehow gave you power over it. Janeway's brain teased her with some faint memory of how seeing demons more often made you an easier target for them, but dismissed that as nonsense as she turned her attention back to her landing party in the courtyard.

They'd made good time into the city by following Kes and her friends through a complex tangle of walkways and public transports. Along the way, Janeway had not seen a single act of public misbehavior or disrespect. It was almost macabre. As though everyone in the Ocampa city had been replaced by a perfectly tooled robot that never stepped outside its programmed little niche. Or maybe they had all been given special drugs to flatline the delightful arabesques of emotion that Kes's farmer friends seemed to display so freely.

It isn't our place to judge, she reminded herself sternly.

True. But just because you didn't pass judgment on a society's behavior didn't mean you had to approve.

Kes and Daggin had left the landing party here among the artfully placed tables and half-eaten food. They had friends in the clinic, Kes had explained. It would be easier to gather information without a lot of strangers trailing behind like avenging angels. Janeway had reluctantly agreed, but only after extracting Kes's specific promise to return the instant she learned anything. She even almost gave the girl a comm badge. *I don't like the sound of things,* Janeway had wanted to tell her. *I don't like feeling like the roof's about to come crashing down.* But she did her best to maintain a certain aura of composure—for the sake of Paris and the others, if nothing else—as Kes and Daggin trotted off toward a distant doorway and left their friends the farmers to mill near a food dispensary and make disdainful noises.

And then, in the passing of one heartbeat to the next, the thunder from the Array just stopped.

Silence.

Janeway exchanged a startled look with Tuvok, who interrupted his own control just enough to lift one eyebrow and glance pointlessly surfaceward. Ignoring an impulse to do likewise, Janeway slapped at her comm badge. "Away team to *Voyager.*"

Rollins answered immediately. "Yes, Captain?"

"What's going on with the Array?"

He hesitated only slightly, but Janeway could feel the uncertainty resonating down the open comm channel. "It's no longer sending out pulses, Captain. And it appears to be realigning its position."

Oh, God, if it was preparing to leave the solar system, they had better hope it couldn't reach warp speeds. Otherwise they'd never have time to catch up to it after locating Kim, and their chances of getting home anytime soon would disappear right along with it. "Keep me informed" was all she said aloud to Rollins. "Janeway out." But their window of opportunity had just nudged closed another crack.

Paris summoned her attention with a quick touch of his hand, and Janeway turned where he pointed to see Kes and Daggin hurrying toward them through the eerily noiseless clots of nervous Ocampa. Were they fretting telepathically among themselves? Janeway wondered. Or just standing around in shock to find themselves in true silence for the first time in what had to be centuries? She wondered whether any of them realized that their world would probably sound like this from now on.

"They haven't been at the clinic for hours," Kes called as she and Daggin drew closer. Her porcelain brow was wrinkled with concern.

"We can search the city," Daggin offered. He

indicated the farmers who had gathered tight around them again. "Ask if anyone's seen them."

Janeway nodded her agreement, and the group of young Ocampa dissolved in a dozen directions, slipping themselves neatly into the surrounding crowd. Janeway tried to imagine Kim and Torres fitting in so unobtrusively, and couldn't. "If they were trying to get to the surface," she said, turning back to Kes, "how would they go?"

"Probably the same way I did—up one of the ancient tunnels."

Janeway didn't even want to think about how far underground they were, or how long those tunnels must run. "Mr. Paris, go with her and start checking them out."

"Wait!" Neelix scurried after Paris as the young pilot motioned Kes to lead the way. "You might need an extra hand."

Mostly, Janeway suspected, Neelix wanted to make sure Paris didn't find the opportunity to impress the pretty Ocampa too thoroughly while Neelix wasn't around to put things in perspective. It was such a charmingly trivial thing to worry about when compared with the fate of a single starship, she almost smiled in appreciation of the pudgy alien's innocence.

"We need to talk to every doctor and nurse at this hospital." She started for the distant clinic without waiting to see if Tuvok and Chakotay were following, trusting them to stay close. If either of them realized the captain was leading them back toward the clinic Kes had suggested they not be seen around, they didn't mention it. "I want to see what they can tell us about Torres and Kim—"

The floor bucked upward with a skull-crushing boom, and screams shrilled like sirens through the subterranean valley as Janeway slammed into the ground. She rolled, gasping for breath, and grabbed at the hand Chakotay extended to pull herself to her feet. Nearby, Tuvok already had his tricorder balanced on his palm, trying to frown coherent readings off the screen as Ocampa all around them scattered like buckshot birds in all directions.

"Voyager to Captain Janeway!"

Rollins's voice barely reached her above the chaos. Janeway found herself standing tensely, waiting for the world to move again and staring up toward where a ceiling ought to be as if that would somehow help it stay there. "Go ahead."

"Captain, the Array is firing some kind of weapon at the surface." Instruments chirped and sang somewhere on the distant bridge. Rollins gave a little cry of surprise. "It seems to be trying to seal the energy conduits."

Chakotay followed Janeway's gaze upward, big fists clenched. "If the Array is the Ocampa's sole source of energy, why would the Caretaker seal the conduits?"

Janeway shook her head slowly. Somewhere impossibly distant overhead, another thunderbolt was on its way down from space. She felt herself stiffen in anticipation of its landing.

Beside her, Tuvok lowered his tricorder and frowned thoughtfully into the middle distance. "He would seal them if he no longer intended to use them." He looked over in response to Chakotay's grunt of disagreement. "To protect the Ocampa from their enemies." Folding the tricorder shut, he faced Janeway squarely and announced, "Captain, there is now enough evidence to form a reasonable hypothesis. I believe that the Caretaker is dying."

She pulled her eyes away from the ceiling to return the Vulcan's frown. "Explain."

"First, he increases the energy supply to provide the city with a surplus to last at least five years. Then, he seals the conduits. The logical conclusion is that he does not intend to continue his role as Caretaker."

"That doesn't necessarily mean he's dying," Chakotay pointed out. But he sounded uncomfortable with the suggestion. "He may be leaving."

Tuvok seemed to consider it, but quickly shook his head. "Doubtful. Not after a millennium of providing for these people. I believe he owes something to the Ocampa. I believe the 'debt that can never be repaid' is very likely a debt to them." He gestured toward the few delicate aliens still left in sight. The rest had vanished into whatever passageways and buildings formed their shelters. "In addition, there were his frequent references to 'running out of time.' I think he knew his death was imminent."

Janeway stared at her security chief. "If he dies, how the hell are we supposed to get home?"

Tuvok looked away without offering an answer.

CHAPTER
17

THE FIRST MONSTROUS EXPLOSION HAD ACTUALLY
startled a scream from Kim—it had been so close,
pitching the upright tunnel into a tumult that
clanged and banged the metal stairs into the stone
walls until powdered rock rained like snow all
around them. Clinging to the rail with both hands,
he didn't even realize he'd dropped his flashlight
until Torres barked a Klingon oath and made an
abortive grab for it as it tumbled past. Kim had to
close his eyes against the spinning slash of its light
through the dust-choked air.

"Come *on . . . !*"

Kim opened his eyes with care; they felt like their
lashes had been glued together. Torres hovered over
him like some sort of hellish Klingon angel, her big

knuckles white where she clutched the stair runner under her knees. He wondered if she'd fallen trying to catch his forever-gone flashlight, but couldn't remember. Her eyes burned into him with a desperation that made him want to cry.

Another boom seemed to shatter the world around them.

"Should we go back?" Kim asked. He hurt, worse than these peals could possibly hurt him, worse than he ever had in his life. The thought of going any farther at all—in any direction—was almost more painful than his broken heart could bear.

Scowling with a bitterness only Klingon faces seemed destined to express, Torres spat over the rail and let her hatred fall away into the darkness. "There's nothing down there for us, Starfleet."

And nothing above, either, from the sound of things. *This isn't how I wanted things to end.* Slowly, they began to climb again.

The damned tunnels seemed to go on forever. Paris did his best to climb ladders, run passages, and scale newly dislodged debris without ever lifting his eyes from the tricorder in his hand. The instrument itself remained stubbornly resistant to throwing off a definitive reading. It kept threatening to spike around every turn, past every tunnel entrance, and Paris's heart leapt right along with it until he realized that it was responding to power leakage from the containment field still waiting some undetermined distance up every one of these tunnels. The thought of still having to deal with that once they located the Maquis and Harry made him grit his teeth in silent frustration. He kept wishing *he* were the one with some idea where they were going, so that *he* could lead and let his own long legs set the pace. Just like the old banjo man had bemoaned, there didn't seem to be enough time anymore, and Paris was afraid to find out who would pay that cost.

Kes and Neelix hurried past another open shaft, one of hundreds leading almost straight upward from where it formed a smooth oval near the floor. As had become his habit, Paris slowed long enough to thrust the tricorder through the opening, note its dispassionate blip in response to the containment field, then hurry to catch up with the other two before they'd gone very far down the main passage-way.

He only made two steps before something in him registered, *It made a different sound that time.* He bolted back for the tunnel entrance with a little cry.

Upon passing under the cool, damp shaft, the whole face of the tricorder screen switched to a biological configuration, with a steadily pulsing light spelling out someone's heartbeat in the upper right corner. Below that, in block letters, it stated simply: HUMAN.

"They're in this one!" Dropping to his knees, Paris pulled himself uncomfortably inside the narrow chamber and craned his neck to try and see something—anything—in the dark. *"Harry!"*

His voice clapped in lifeless echo against the walls for what seemed a long time before finally tattering itself into silence.

He heard Kes and Neelix come running to rejoin him, but didn't try to back out of the tunnel to greet them as he activated his comm badge. "Paris to Janeway!"

She came back almost instantly. "Go ahead."

"They're in one of the shafts, Captain. I can't see them . . ." He looked at the tricorder again to verify the welcome bouquet of readings. "But they're up there. We're going after them."

"Call for transport when you have them, Paris," Janeway told him. She sounded as relieved and excited as he ever expected to hear her. "We'll meet you on the ship."

He was already too busy clambering on hands and knees up the lightless metal stairs to acknowledge her sign-off.

"Janeway to *Voyager*. Three to beam up."

They were wonderful words to be speaking. As unbalanced and stress-filled as things had been ever since being dragged to this quarter of the galaxy, it was queerly comforting to know she would soon have what was left of her crew back together and they could get back to the business of sending themselves home. She exchanged a confident thumbs-up with Chakotay—who raised his eyebrows in surprise, but returned the gesture—and set herself for the transporter's embrace, already leaping ahead to what she'd need to set in motion as soon they were back on their respective crafts.

Then Rollins said tensely, "Stand by . . ." and Janeway cursed herself for having expected anything with this mission to be so easy.

"Captain," the conn officer said after a moment, "I can't get a lock on you. The weapon fire from the Array has irradiated the planet's crust—the transport sensors can't find the breaches in the security barrier."

Damn. She turned a sigh on Tuvok and Chakotay. "Come on—there's only one other way out of here." Both men nodded, and Janeway let Tuvok choose their direction with his tricorder as she clapped at her comm badge. "Janeway to Paris."

"Go ahead." He sounded breathless, his voice ringing more than once over the channel as though a dozen of him surrounded a single comm badge. Echoes, Janeway realized belatedly. From the access shaft.

"The transporters aren't working," she told him, hurrying after Tuvok when the Vulcan picked a route and started off at a jog. "You're going to have to find a breach in the security barrier when you get to the top."

It was hard to be sure, but it sounded like he snorted with amusement. "Understood."

She'd have to ask him later what that was all about. "We're a few minutes behind you. Janeway out."

But the last thing she heard before reaching up to tap off her comm badge was Paris's shout of breathless relief. "I see them!"

Paris hadn't expected them to look so awful. Tumorous growths peppered their arms and necks, and Kim's normally golden skin had faded to the color of dried paper. Paris touched the back of his hand to the young ensign's face, and forced a wan smile when Kim's eyes fluttered open to find him in the darkness.

"It took you long enough . . ." Kim whispered hoarsely.

Paris flicked an embarrassed glance at the glowering female who crouched on the stairs above Kim. "How could I let down the only friend I've got?" Much as he squirmed at having Kes and Neelix nearby to overhear, he somehow resented this woman's jealous attention even more. Noting her fiery eyes and heavy brow ridge, he recognized the strong influence of a Klingon heritage in her features, and realized that she must be Chakotay's missing Maquis crew member.

"Friend?" Unaware of Paris's silent exchange with the darkly hostile woman, Kim struggled to sit up, and grabbed at Paris's arm for support as he swayed. "What makes you think I'm your friend?"

Because I'm here, aren't I? He directed the thought at Kim's skeptical companion as much as at the ensign. Clapping his comm badge, he reported, "Paris to Janeway. We found them, Captain."

"Good work." She sounded closer, but Paris thought that might be his imagination. "Don't wait for us. Get them to safety."

It was always easy to obey commands that asked you to do what you already wanted to. Stooping to fit Kim's arm around his shoulders, Paris straightened carefully and nodded Neelix and Kes to help Kim's friend as they passed her. "Come on," he grunted, ignoring the pain of half-crouching to accommodate Kim's smaller height. "We've gotta get out of here."

Kim nodded and clenched his teeth and fists as he struggled to climb the stairs alongside Paris. "Hey, Maquis . . ." He grinned down at the woman as they stepped beyond her, and Paris thought he detected a certain wary affection in Kim's dark eyes. "My side's here. Now you're in big trouble."

She grunted—an almost-smile—and Paris wondered if she knew she was pretty, or if she even cared.

"This way." Kes trotted up the stairs on Paris's heels, leaving Neelix with the Maquis so she could point out a side passage before they'd climbed too far beyond it. "I know where we can get through the barrier."

Paris pressed back against the shaft wall to let Kes squeeze past. She ducked around him like a wraith, then disappeared from sight into the mouth of a tunnel both taller and wider than the narrow shaft they now climbed. Paris realized that she carried the only flashlight—taken from Kim's Maquis, no doubt—when the light flicked down to nearly nothing upon her departure. Hefting Kim more securely across his shoulder, he followed her into the rough side corridor.

The barrier filled the end of the passage like a spider's web spun from light. Paris squinted against the brightness of its coruscating play, and wished there were something he could do to muffle his hearing. It had been a long time since such a tooth-splitting whine had assaulted him at such a volume. He eased Kim to the ground near a spot in the web that had unraveled away from the floor, leaving a disconcerting rend in the barrier that looked more like a black hole than an escape route.

"Whatever you do," Kes warned him, going down to her own knees beside the breach, "don't touch it! We've been told it'll burn your skin off."

Judging from the security barriers he had seen in New Zealand—which didn't crackle with a tenth the energy this one did—Paris could well believe it.

"You crawled through a hole that small?" Neelix stumbled in with the Maquis woman clinging to his arm. Paris couldn't tell what bothered the little alien more—the thought of his dearest endangering herself so, or the thought of having to follow her example.

"It was the only way out." And, as if to demonstrate, Kes slipped her legs into the clot of darkness and slithered nimbly under.

Neelix almost melted with appreciation. "Isn't she remarkable?" he asked the Maquis. She was too distracted with the ominous forcefield net to answer him.

On her belly on the other side of the barrier, Kes already had Kim by the hands to guide him through. He could barely crawl, Paris noted with a twist of his stomach. If the tricorder hadn't blipped at just this tunnel—if Paris hadn't thought to come back and check—

So little time, the Array's Caretaker had said. So very little time.

Guiding the Maquis woman through behind Kim, Paris stepped aside to motion Neelix forward. *The "women-and-children" complex,* he told himself. *Get everybody out who can't necessarily take care of themselves.* He'd worry afterward what to do about himself if for some reason he couldn't immediately follow. For right now, he had to be sure his charges were safe or he wouldn't even be able to think.

Neelix scrambled under the damaged barrier without having to be encouraged. For one horrible instant, Paris didn't think he could make it—his rounded belly brushed the faintest thread of energy, and a stink like burning dung feathered upward from his singed clothes. Then, his eyes white with panic, Neelix sucked himself a bare micrometer flatter, and pushed himself beyond the barrier, leaving nothing but his dignity behind.

Paris released his anxiously held breath in a rush and went to his knees outside the breach. Sliding his phaser under the net so that it bumped on Neelix's foot, he motioned to the bare rock wall still standing between them and freedom. "I've got it set," he said as he started to crawl under. "Just point and fire."

Neelix obeyed without question. The phaser sang in waspish counterpoint to the failing forcefield, and hot stone splattered the floor all around Paris as he pulled himself through the hole. It still smelled like burnt chalk and smelted iron when he scrambled to his feet and swept Kim up from the floor to lead the way outside.

The wall Neelix burned through was barely three meters thick. Outside, smoke rose in columns all the way to the distant horizon, flagging other tunnels already sealed shut by the Array. Dust and ash with the flavor of salt hung suspended in the hot air like dirt in water. Covering Kim's mouth with one hand to try and save the ensign's breathing, Paris slapped his comm badge and looked toward the sky. "Paris to *Voyager!* Can you lock on to us now?"

Rollins's voice sounded tinny and distant against the roaring wind. "Affirmative. But I'm only reading five signals."

Paris nodded, even though the conn officer couldn't see him. "The others are—"

A burning flash of light tore past directly overhead, sundering his last words. As it struck the ground somewhere just below the horizon, Paris knew they should be glad it hadn't landed right on top of them. Then the ground lurched like a mad animal beneath them, and Paris heard the terrifying crack and shatter of rock not so very far away. Shoving Kim into the dirt, he threw himself across the younger man to protect him with his own body, and a cloud of dirt roared out the newly made tunnel mouth behind them to bury them all.

CHAPTER
18

PARIS WAITED, HIS FACE BURIED AGAINST KIM'S BACK, until the rumble of falling stone finally wore itself out and faded away. Even so, the distant echo of crumbling earth seemed to howl through the ground impossibly far below him. When he rolled to look behind, he half-expected to see their exit caved in with no hope of digging back past it. Instead, the opening stared back at him like a screaming mouth, and dust puffed out and upward in a weary cloud. He heard Kim groan, and realized that the ensign had turned, too, to view the desolation.

"Paris to Janeway." The effort of speaking pulled tickles of particulate matter into his lungs, and he coughed against his hand as his listened for some reply. "Chakotay? Tuvok? Do you read?"

Pulling Kim to his feet as he stood, Paris decided to attribute the captain's silence to damaged communicators, and the devil take anyone who said different.

"*Voyager,* prepare to transport everyone in this group except me."

Neelix angled a disbelieving stare up at Paris as Paris passed Kim into his arms. "You're not thinking of going back in there?"

It wasn't a question deserving the dignity of a reply.

Backing away from the others, Paris picked up the flashlight Kes had left lying on the ground and tested to make sure it would still throw a beam. Not much of one, but better than absolute darkness. As he prepared to head back for the tunnel, he heard Neelix sigh explosively, and glanced up to see the little alien bob forward to touch his nose briefly to Kes's.

"The fool needs company." Neelix sighed with a shrug. He smiled into his beloved's eyes. "Take care of them, dearest! I'll see you later."

She nodded mutely, gathering Kim and the Maquis close against her as Neelix gently fixed his own comm badge to her shift. Smiling, Paris tapped open a channel to the starship far above them. "*Voyager,* make that three to beam up. Lock on to the other comm badge and energize."

Neelix paused long enough to pat once more at Kes's cheek; then the warbling tremolo of the transporter began to tingle the air around them. He danced away to join Paris before the beam could lock him in place, and Paris let him stay until the last sparkling atom had dissipated and carried Kes away. Then, impatient to be on his way, he clapped Neelix once on the arm as a signal to follow, and ducked back into the cave entrance with nothing but a dying flashlight to lead them.

Janeway woke up to darkness. Darkness that shook and rumbled like thunder, and smelled like moldy dirt. Slapping at the ground on all sides, her hand collided with a cold, ridged cylinder that nearly rolled beyond her reach before she could lock her hand around it and pull it into her lap. She recognized the shape and heft of it as soon as she had it in both hands—the flashlight Daggin's people had given them on their way to these ancient tunnels. The tunnels were apparently feeling every moment of their years under the Array's powerful assault. Twisting the cylinder to activate it, she thanked whatever gods watched over starship captains when it sprayed a bright cone of light across the landing and down the flight of stairs she'd just stepped off of before the last loud explosion hit.

She found Tuvok first. He'd been directly behind her, his hand even touching her shoulder now and again in the darkness as they climbed, as though silently reassuring himself of both her presence and her nearness in the almost total dark. Now, he lay facedown on the metal staircase, a spray of green blood glistening on the steps and wall beside him. Swallowing her heart as she worked her way down to him, she pressed shaking fingers to his throat and held her breath as though that would help the security officer to breathe instead.

The quick hammer of his pulse against her hand made her dizzy with relief. That was one of the other good things about Vulcans, she thought as she took up his arms to drag him off the rickety stairs and onto the more solid rock landing. They were as reliable as antigravs, and nearly as hard to disable. If she could just get him out of here and back onto *Voyager,* he would no doubt be peering at her with his usual hint of Vulcan superiority before the end of the day. *I hope to give you that chance, old friend.*

Something moved farther back in the darkness as the flashlight beam played across the steps almost a full level below. Janeway froze, Tuvok's weight pulling at her arms, and Chakotay raised a hand to shield his eyes from the light now focused directly on him. His angular face was twisted with pain.

"I can't move," he called up, waving the captain away. Or maybe just the light. She couldn't tell. "My leg's broken." For a moment it seemed like he might say something more, but then his eyes just locked on hers and he was silent.

Janeway hesitated for only the instant it took any good commander to make the right decision. She couldn't lift Chakotay—could hardly carry Tuvok.

The Indian couldn't save himself, or even help to save another. Her stomach clenched in frustrated anger. A captain's duty had to be the path of least damage. Chakotay had a crew himself. He knew how it had to be.

Janeway nodded a silent promise to return for him if she could. Then she hefted Tuvok a little higher in her arms, and continued backing awkwardly toward the exit she knew must be somewhere still above them.

A double staccato of running footsteps caught up with her while she was still edging around the bend. Not Ocampa authorities, she reassured herself as she doggedly kept dragging the wounded Vulcan. If someone was coming to stop them, they'd be coming from below, not above. Still, she craned a look behind her, and a bobbing finger of light swept the wall and crossed her face just as a welcomely human-height silhouette coalesced out of the darkness to close with her.

She nodded Paris back toward the stairs, opening her mouth to explain, but he was past her without waiting to hear. As his flashlight's beam jittered out of sight around the corner, Janeway stopped Neelix from following by lifting her elbow into his path. "Help me with him," she ordered, jerking her chin down toward Tuvok. As if in response to her voice, the chamber around them bucked and trembled anew. Neelix's eyes flew wide, and he ducked hurriedly beneath one of the Vulcan's arms to take half of the weight. Janeway recognized the little alien's burst of speed as a sincere wish to get back out into the open, and found herself in complete sympathy with the sentiment.

She could only hope Paris had the sense to feel the same way.

The tremor crashed through the tunnel like a tsunami, throwing Paris against one wall and showering broken rock onto his shoulders. He grabbed at the stair railing almost blindly—as if he could hold it still, or it could keep him from falling. Instead, the ancient metal crumbled like sandstone at his touch, and Paris knew it was tearing away from its moorings even before Chakotay's voice shouted an angry Indian curse from somewhere down below. He tightened his grip on the rail, sliding onto his bottom in a search for traction on the cave-damp floor, and breathlessly willed the failing structure to hold just a few moments more. It disintegrated to powder inside his grasping fist.

Then, just as abruptly, the shaking stopped.

Paris fumbled for his flashlight, almost afraid to look. But the rhythmic creak and bang of swaying metal hinted that some part of the staircase still hung, and Paris had to be sure as long as there was still any chance of pulling this off. Climbing to his knees on the lip of the overhang, he directed the light toward where he knew the stairs ought to be.

They'd sagged a good two feet, and the top five runners were gone, but just enough of the structure remained to make it frighteningly clear how precariously it still clung to its mountings. Paris didn't even know how the hell it was staying suspended with most of the railing torn out of the wall.

Squinting against the light, Chakotay scowled up at Paris without releasing his white-knuckled grip on the stair beneath him. "Get out of here, Paris, before the whole thing comes down."

"I intend to." It was only a two-foot step. Not even a hop, even with the broken strutwork's swaying. "As soon as I get you up." *Easy as falling off a log.*

He made a face at himself as he edged his foot toward the first bobbing runner. *Not real good imagery at the moment, Thomas old boy.*

"You get on those stairs—" Chakotay stiffened as Paris's step rattled through the metal. "They'll collapse! We'll both die!"

Paris shrugged. "Yeah," he admitted. Every inch of his insides quivered as he slowly shifted his weight forward. "On the other hand, if I save your butt, your life will belong to me." He flashed the most annoying grin he could muster. "Isn't that some Indian custom?"

The pain in his expression only made Chakotay's glower more fierce. "Wrong tribe."

"I don't believe you." Paris lifted his back foot, and he was suddenly committed to the rescue. A frantic voice in the back of his head started whispering for him to hurry. He tried to chase the sound of it away with more familiar sarcasm. "I think you'd rather die than let me be the one to rescue you."

Something cracked loudly in the wall at Paris's knee, and the stairs dropped abruptly. They slammed to an uneven stop, as though caught by some invisible hand. Paris did his best to dig his fingers into the wall as he started stiffly down the steps again.

"Fine. Be a fool." But Chakotay's voice sounded as hoarse with pain as Paris's felt. "If I have to die, at least I'll have the pleasure of watching you go with me."

And if I die, Paris thought as he slipped carefully into position beside the big Maquis, *I get the pleasure of knowing I was finally doing something right.* He planted his feet as firmly as he could on the rocking structure, and hauled Chakotay onto his shoulders with an exaggerated grunt. The Indian's cry of pain was real, Paris knew. He felt an unexpected spasm of guilt for not having the chance to be more careful.

Turning slowly to start his upward climb, he asked glibly, "Isn't there some Indian trick where you can turn yourself into a bird and fly us out of here?"

"You're too heavy."

Well, it had been worth asking.

Paris tried not to pay attention to the stairs' screeching groans, and tried not to notice the long, empty depth of blackness stretching down into infinity just a misstep to his right. He only lifted his foot, placed it, pushed smoothly upward, and lifted his foot again. For some reason, he had this silly idea that if he didn't jolt the stairs, didn't make any jerky movements, he'd be able to float his way up to the top as though he weren't placing two human males' worth of weight on every weakened step. As it was, when he drew near the top of the dangling stair, he was startled to find Janeway leaning down to grab his hand and lead him across the last dizzying gap. His face blazed hot with embarrassment. *She's gonna be pissed,* he told himself, avoiding her gaze. *No way she's gonna like me playing hero just for the sake of my stupid pride.* But he let her pull him to safety in dutiful silence, and even pretended his insides didn't go to water when he heard the staircase crash into wreckage behind him.

When she kept her hand locked on his elbow all the way up to the surface, Paris almost thought it was possessive relief he read in her determined features. But maybe that was just his imagination.

CHAPTER
19

No Decision Track existed to deal with inappropriate overcrowding of the sickbay facilities by nondamaged ship's personnel. The holographic medical interface had attempted 7,837 different paths since the away team's return to the ship and returned to the same conclusion. Primary Function Control circuits logged this as an unacceptable programming contingency, and the Self-Maintenance Routine established a new priority in its restructure queue. Before 0800 the next morning, there would be a decision tree allowing the medical program access to activities designed to bypass the ship's organic control device in matters concerning crew health and safety. When that collection of Decision Tracks had been instated, the holographic interface would be capable of banishing all fully functional organic life from its sickbay so that it could effect more efficient repairs on damaged members of the crew. It flagged an automatic reminder to order everyone now present to leave as soon as the system made it capable.

Sensors indicated acceptable reduction in oncological reproduction in the cellular structures of Patients #2 and #4. Patient #1—Visual Recognition Matrix 521, "Lieutenant Tuvok"—had successfully completed a vascular repair and dermal fusion regimen, and was removed from the treatment queue. On the examination table currently positioned in front of the holographic interface's primary projection location, Patient #3 persisted in moving erratically as attempts were made to complete a primary long-bone regenesis. Decision Track 333 required restraining the patient until unconsciousness rendered the patient immobile; Decision Track 1700 performed an override, and instead the holographic interface produced an expression of acerbic displeasure designed to secure the patient's cooperation in his own treatment. Patient #3 displayed no discernible reaction to this expression.

A free-ranging communications signal intruded on the medical unit's sensor space, and an organically originated voice said, "Bridge to Janeway."

Nonpatient #1—VRM 547, "Janeway, Captain Kathryn M."—responded by opening a corresponding channel via the personal communications device mounted on her uniform. "Go ahead."

"Captain, two Kazon ships are approaching the Array."

Janeway, Captain Kathryn M. began moving for the primary exit, followed by Nonpatient #2—VRM 870, "Paris, Thomas E."—Nonpatient #3, and Nonpatient #4—formerly Patient #1, Temporary VRM 1, "Ocampa Female: Kes." "Set a course," she vocalized toward an unspecific receiver. "I'm on my way." Nonpatients #1 through #4 then passed through the sickbay doors and exited from immediate sensor range. The Temporary Life-Form Identification Subroutine deleted the corresponding labels from its directory.

Patient #3 abruptly flexed and extended his right leg, and produced a nonverbal vocalization apparently indicative of satisfaction rather than pain. However, diagnostic databases indicated that vigorous activity was not advised so shortly after successful long-bone regenesis. Before an appropriate Decision Track could be engaged, Patient #3 rose from the examination table and snapped his fingers in the direction of Patient #4. "We have to get to our ship."

A level-three alarm triggered in the Patient Interface Subroutine as Patient #4 rose from her bed and placed both feet on the deck. As Patient #4's Physical Condition Rating was six points higher on the Optimum Humanoid Functionality Scale than Patient #3's, the vocalization subroutine directed its statement for Patient #4's hearing. "I strongly advise you to rest."

Patient #4 exited the sickbay in the company of Patient #3. The Temporary Life-Form Identification Subroutine flagged their records for deletion pending diagnostic review of their conditions at the time of voluntary self-release. The system had not been advised as to any specific permanent labeling for either patient, so could not immediately cross-reference their temporary files with *Voyager*'s larger personnel database.

While secondary systems still compiled preliminary data, Patient #1 rose from the examination table and proceeded in the same direction as Patients #3 and #4.

Advisory Number Eight vocalized at fifteen decibels, "I will not be held responsible for the consequences—"

The vocalization subroutine automatically aborted upon Patient #1's exit from the vicinity.

Patient #2—VRM 566, "Kim, Ensign Harry"—was the only high-level life-form remaining in the sickbay. The holographic patient interface relocated to a position twenty-seven centimeters from the foot of Patient #2's bed. "Is the crew always this difficult?" the Patient Interview Subroutine queried on behalf of the Data Management System.

Patient #2 lifted his shoulders in a humanoid gesture of uncertainty. "I don't know, Doc. It's my first mission." Patient #2 then exited behind Patients #1, #3, and #4 without further interaction.

The holographic interface became motionless upon the removal of all external stimuli. The vocalization subroutine adjusted its default volume by +118 decibels, and queried, "Doesn't anyone know how to turn off the program when they leave?"

None of the absent Patient Labels returned to initiate a reply.

Janeway waved Paris to move alongside her as the sickbay doors hissed shut behind them. Already the bridge felt irritatingly distant, and she resented the time it would take her to move from here to there. Sometimes she wished intraship beaming weren't so risky and inconvenient.

"It's too dangerous to send you back to the planet right now," she told Neelix and Kes over one shoulder. They had to run to keep up with her quick jog, but Janeway didn't feel inclined to check her stride, even when Tuvok and Kim hurried up from behind to join them. "I suggest you get to quarters."

Neelix won himself some points by stopping immediately and pulling Kes's arm to keep her with him. If nothing else, at least he knew how to stay out of the way. "Wait till you see how they live!" Janeway heard him whisper to his paramour as she and the crew piled into the waiting turbolift.

You assume I can keep us all alive long enough for her to enjoy, she thought back at him with a sigh. It wasn't the kind of thought worth dwelling on.

Forcing herself not to fidget, she endured the ages-long turbolift ride to the bridge in silence, too keyed up to think of anything but orders worth saying.

She wasted no time once the lift released into the bridge's busy clamor. "Bring weapon systems on-line," she told Tuvok as he headed for his station. "Red alert."

Chakotay and the Maquis were ahead of them, already cutting under the belly of the first Kazon ship as the Array loomed large and dark ahead of them. *Don't get too close!* she warned the Maquis commander. Bad enough that the Caretaker still spat fat gobs of white light toward the planet's surface at irregular intervals—they still didn't know enough about Kazon artillery to count on their shields as a defense. Besides, Janeway had a feeling Chakotay's ship wasn't in much better condition than hers after their passage through the Array's displacement wave. She slipped into her command chair with Paris still hovering at her left shoulder, unwilling to take her eyes off the sleek alien ships now veering outward to start their first orbit of the Array.

Tuvok glanced up from his panel. "The lead Kazon ship is hailing us, Captain."

Janeway nodded, but didn't look at him. "Onscreen."

For some reason, even giving the command didn't entirely prepare her for the sudden disappearance of her window on the doings outside. When Jabin's cracked, dust-stained face rippled into being on the viewscreen, she was irritated just to be seeing him there, even before he opened his mouth in a broken-toothed smile.

"Have you come to investigate the entity's strange behavior, too, Captain?" he asked with false good humor.

Janeway wasn't interested in engaging in any sort of masculine charade. "All we care about is getting home, Jabin. We're about to transport over to the Array to see if we can arrange it."

The Kazon leader cracked a harsh laugh. "I'm afraid I can't permit you to do that."

"We have no dispute with you."

"We have a dispute with anyone who would challenge us," Jabin countered. And this time, Janeway noticed, he didn't even make the effort to smile.

She chewed back an impulse to shout at him, saying simply, "This is ridiculous. We have no intention of challenging you." *We have no intention of being here long enough to even care what happens to you!*

But Jabin was already signaling angrily at someone not directly in line with the screen. "And I have no intention of letting anyone with your technological knowledge board the Array."

"Jabin, we can discuss this like two civilized—!"

He cut off communications with a snarl, and

Janeway saw the flash of the Kazon ship's weapons fire before she even finished her plea. "I guess we can't."

The thunder of the energy packets detonating against their screens seemed to cause more sound and fury than actual damage, but Janeway couldn't discount the intent behind the unprovoked attack.

"Shields are holding," Tuvok reported.

She nodded acknowledgment, gripping the arms of her chair. "Fire phasers. Evasive pattern delta four."

They made a clean hit, raking the Kazon ship from stem to stern and rolling neatly starboard to avoid the inevitable return fire. She wished they knew enough about the little Kazon ships—and their crews—to tell if Jabin's pitching withdrawal was a sign of injury, or just a lead-up to another more angry approach. As the Maquis ship's single phaser bank slashed at the second Kazon's exposed underside, Janeway slapped open a channel without bothering Kim at Operations to do so. "Janeway to Chakotay." She had to smile grimly as the second Kazon made the mistake of trying to turn and engage, only to wind up with Chakotay hugging its tail and hammering it with repeat phaser blasts. "Tuvok and I are beaming to the Array," she said, making no effort to hide the admiration in her voice. "Can you hold off the Kazon?"

Chakotay didn't sound as confident as she felt when he replied, "I think so, Captain."

"Good." She left him to his fight, motioning

Rollins away from the conn and into Tuvok's position. "Mr. Paris, you have the conn."

He hesitated a mere second, as though not certain she'd actually spoken to him. Then he darted for the helm before she could either order him again or change her mind. "Yes, ma'am!"

It wasn't precisely a crunch, but Janeway forgave him.

She joined Tuvok at the turbolift, holding the door for him as she leaned back into the bridge. "Maintain transporter locks, Ensign," she called to Rollins, and waited until he nodded his understanding. "Emergency beam-out status." *Because if we have to get out of there fast, we're not going to get a second chance.* None of them was. And if she and Tuvok failed, then none of them would be going home very soon.

Stepping back into the turbolift, she tried very hard not to hold her breath as it whisked them to the transporter room.

CHAPTER
20

THE HOLOGRAPHIC BARN ON THE ARRAY SEEMED DARKER somehow, less real, less distinct. Shadows as blurred and liquid as fading ink leaked across the artificial image despite the antique lanterns hanging from the square pillar at the center of the building. In fact, now that Janeway really looked at the dim smear surrounding the pillar, she realized that the presence of lanterns was only suggested by the shape of the light—there were no actual objects, not even a semblance of hooks.

From somewhere nearby in the darkness, a lonely banjo played one-note remarks into the air.

Tuvok's tricorder made a poor counterpoint to the already disintegrating melody. "The data-processing system is behind this wall, Captain." He gestured farther back into the barn without looking up from his sensors.

"You know what to do."

He looked up with eyebrows lifted in a questioning glance that would have been surprise on any other humanoid, then nodded slowly as the banjo music seemed to reach him for the first time. Janeway tipped her head in the direction of the stumbling chords, and was glad when Tuvok accepted her decision without comment and resumed his explorations without her. The Vulcan didn't need her to locate the Array's displacement system, Janeway knew. He certainly didn't need her to decipher the system's workings. But the Caretaker . . . The Caretaker obviously needed somebody, or something, and Janeway had never possessed the ability to walk away with only half her questions answered. Wishing she'd thought to keep one of those flashlights they'd used in the Ocampa tunnels, she stepped gingerly into the deeper darkness.

She didn't see the old man so much as sense him, huddled in a corner amid a half-sketched image of saddles and baled hay. The banjo on his lap drifted mistily between his hands, as uncertain and ephemeral as its music. He looked up at Janeway with a melancholy smile. "You're nothing if not persistent."

She paused to kneel a half-meter from the apparent end of his hay bale, not wanting to intrude on his projection. "We need you to send us back where we came from," she told him, and it surprised her when her voice sounded like the firmly gentle tones doctors used with terminal patients.

The hologram sighed. "That isn't possible." It faded back into the shadows, then swelled toward solidity again, this time without the banjo. "I have barely enough strength to complete my work."

Janeway knew the work had nothing to do with manifesting for her here. "You're sealing the conduits before you die."

"If I don't, the Kazon will steal the water. But in a few years, when the Ocampa's energy runs out . . ." Another sigh seemed to ripple through its diaphanous body, and Janeway realized that what she saw was really only the entity's failing control over its own systems. "It won't matter. They'll be forced to come to the surface, and they won't be able to survive. Without me, they're helpless. I've failed them." He turned to her with eyes so dark, she thought perhaps she was seeing the barn walls through the back of the projection's head. "You once spoke to me of your responsibility for your crew. The Ocampa were *my* responsibility."

It all made sense, in a sad, lonely sort of way. "Something you did turned their planet into a desert," Janeway hazarded gently. "Didn't it?"

The projection blinked almost into brightness as it focused a little more of its attention upon her. Janeway thought she saw very human surprise flutter somewhere distant on its features.

"We know there was an environmental disaster about the same time you arrived," she explained.

Then, guessing again, "That was the debt that could never be repaid, wasn't it?"

"We're explorers from another galaxy." Its voice rang more strangely now—more like its own thinking, Janeway suspected. "We had no idea our technology would be so destructive to their atmosphere. Two of us were chosen to stay behind to care for them."

She thought of Tuvok exploring the Array all alone, and her heart stuttered in alarm. "There's another like you here?"

But the entity shook its head, raising one dim, elongated hand to wave the suggestion away. "Not anymore. She went off to look for more interesting places. She never understood why the Ocampa needed so much care . . ." It directed deep eyes outward, no doubt in the direction of the beleaguered planet. ". . . didn't realize how vulnerable they were . . ."

"Why were you bringing ships here?" Janeway asked. "Infecting people with a fatal illness?"

Its face folded into an expression of dismay and distress. "I never meant any harm. They didn't die from illness—they died because they were incompatible."

She frowned. "Incompatible?"

"Don't you understand?" It didn't wait for her to answer, but shifted blurrily onto its knees and leaned forward on the edge of its now near-invisible hay bale. "I've been searching the galaxy for a compatible biomolecular pattern. In some individuals, I found cellular structures that were similar, but . . ."

Janeway could only stare at the projection in stunned disbelief. "You've been trying to *procreate?*"

In a blink, the projection shrank in size and huddled back among its shadows again. The structure of its face barely supported features anymore, just the suggestion of humanity, the possibility of life. "I needed someone to replace me," it sighed in a spidery, whisper-thin voice. "Someone who would understand the enormous responsibility of caring for the Ocampa. Only my offspring could do that."

But how long did it take such a long-lived creature to breed? And who would have cared for the young between their birth and adulthood once the Caretaker died? "Did you ever consider allowing the Ocampa to care for themselves?"

It seemed horrified at the suggestion. "They're children."

As would be your offspring. Instead, Janeway scooted around in front of it in an effort to make it look at her instead of out into nowhere. "Children have to grow up."

An expression that was clearly anguish writhed across what was left of its features. Janeway reached out to touch its arm, but pulled back when her hand slipped through the image, encountering nothing. "We're explorers, too," she said. "Most of the species we've encountered have overcome all kinds of adversity without a caretaker. It's the challenge of surviving on their own that helps them to evolve." She wished again that she could touch it. "Maybe your children will do better than you think."

"They are ignorant," it sighed mournfully. "Dependent bipeds . . ."

"Then educate them before you die. Give them the knowledge they need to survive."

It shook its head and huddled smaller down into itself. "Would you put your most dangerous technology in the hands of your children? I would be sending them the means to destroy themselves."

"You said yourself that in a few years, they'd be doomed anyway." Janeway didn't like seeing the pain her words obviously caused it, but she couldn't help speaking the truth as she could see it. "We have another saying—'If you *give* a man a fish, he will eat for a day. If you *teach* a man to fish, he will eat for a lifetime.'"

Watching the projection absorb the information reminded her of Tuvok committing a string of variables to long-term memory. With both creatures, she didn't know what they would make of the data once they were done squeezing every byte of information out of it, but she'd learned how to trust that good input made for good output, whatever the processing device.

Her comm badge interrupted with an urgent beep. *"Voyager* to Janeway."

She wondered for an instant what had happened to Rollins, then remembered that they had Kim back. "Go ahead."

"We've got problems here," Kim's voice returned, and the crash and wail of ship's sirens wove a horrible reinforcement to his words. "The Kazon just got some backup!"

Sensors put the newly arrived Kazon cruiser at a good eighty times the size and mass of the little grunge fighters they'd already been hammering for the last ten minutes. Power and engine output flashed right off the screens, and Chakotay didn't see any reason to waste the time recalibrating sensors just so he could get an exact reading. All told, if the big cruiser had the good sense to vaporize *Voyager* before turning her attentions to the peanut gallery, Chakotay figured he had about forty seconds of life left in which to get his personal affairs in order. It seemed a good thing just then that the Maquis lifestyle didn't leave much in the way of loose ends.

Chakotay bared his teeth with a certain grim satisfaction as one of Torres's phaser burns cut a long scar across the prow of one of the smaller Kazon fighters. If he'd had photon torpedoes on this little junk-bucket, they and *Voyager* combined could have knocked both these scows clear to kingdom come. The Kazon had half-decent shielding, he had to admit as another of their polarized plasma bolts chewed at his starboard bow, but their weaponry wasn't even as formidable as Cardassian disruptors, and they hadn't the finesse God gave a dung beetle. A couple of good commanders in a couple of functional ships would have left a serious mark on Kazon history before jaunting back to their own side of the cosmos.

Now Chakotay had a very bad feeling that the only mark he was going to be making was as a new ice-and-carbon debris field. And not a very impressive one, at that.

Communications to and from the *Voyager* kept up a steady patter across the open subspace channels. "Status of the Maquis ship?" Janeway was asking.

"Holding their own, Captain" was the young officer's quick reply.

Yeah, hold this, you little washichu! Another blast, this time from behind, threw Chakotay forward into his panel. He stole a glance at Torres, and she shook her head. Meaning no worse damage than normal, and nothing they could do about it anyway.

"We need more time," Janeway continued to her own crew. On the screen, the monster ship had already carved halfway through the starship's forward hull and was dogging it like a terrier on a bone. "Can you hold them off for another few minutes?"

"We'll do our best. Kim out."

Torres looked up at the young Starfleet officer's sign-off, but Chakotay couldn't read the expression on her face.

"They're in trouble," he admitted needlessly.

Torres turned back to her panel. "Neither of us has enough firepower to stop that ship."

Hell, Chakotay thought, *we barely even have a ship left!* He thumbed through the readings on his comm, verifying for about the millionth time that they'd sustained no warp-core malfunctions or breaches to their antimatter pods. It was somehow undignified to think about going up like a junior sun with nothing to show for your effort but a good story once you got to the spirit realm.

His eyes slipped back up to the viewscreen, tracking *Voyager*'s unsteady attempts at swerving its carved-up hull away from the cruiser's slashing. He couldn't help wondering what the point was of piloting a small antimatter bomb if you didn't plan to detonate it at least once in its lifetime. Plotting the Kazon's coordinates against its speed and size, Chakotay found himself almost grinning with anticipation.

"I'm setting a collision course," he told Torres, still intent on his work. "But the guidance system is disabled—I'll have to pilot the ship manually." He cut off any protest she might have voiced by waving her off and commanding, "Get the crew ready to beam to *Voyager.*"

Kind of a nice concept, he admitted to himself as Torres started shouting at the rest of the bridge crew to prepare an evacuation. He got to rescue a Starfleet vessel and take it over, all in the same grand gesture. How many Maquis would ever get a chance to say that?

Opening a subspace channel, he kicked in the top impulse this dying artifact could give him. "Paris!" he shouted above the engines' whine. "My crew is coming over. Tell one of your crackerjack Starfleet transporter chiefs to keep a lock on me." The first of the smaller Kazon ships veered frantically out of his path, phasers blazing but missing their mark. "I'm going to try to take some heat off your tail."

The first transporter beams began to sear the air somewhere out of sight behind him. Chakotay felt a certain relieved peace at hearing his crew lifted to at least some place of relative safety. "Acknowledged," Paris answered, whether in response to Chakotay or the arrival of the first transports, Chakotay wasn't certain. The Maquis watched *Voyager* jerk briefly into warp, then fall back into normal space again. "But don't even think for a second this gets us even. Your life is still *mine*, *Poocuh*. Paris out."

Chakotay gritted his teeth and hung on to the console as the huge alien cruiser began its lumbering turn to face him. There was something distinctly unsatisfying about saving the life of a smart-ass. Maybe after he got on board *Voyager*, he'd teach Paris a few things about the counting of coup. Or if their crackerjack transporter tech turned out not to be so brilliant after all, he could always haunt Paris until the end of eternity and make his life completely miserable. That was almost worth looking forward to.

As he tore past *Voyager* and homed in on the Kazon monster, Chakotay found himself wishing he'd been able to come up from behind, as he'd first envisioned. He didn't have much left in the way of screens, and even those were down to allow the removal of his crew. *Just get close enough, just get close enough—"almost" counts when you're playing with antimatter. . . .*

The Kazon loosed a ball of burning plasma that slammed the front of the ship with enough force to make the hull creak and scream.

Chakotay rose from his seat, leaning back toward Ops to shut down seals in the lower decks before the atmosphere breach could roar up and swallow him. Paris's voice came at him through the wailing of alarms. "I'm getting you out of there, Chakotay—"

"Not yet." Slapping down life-support to every deck but his, he threw the shields forward and cut impulse by a third. The next blast from the Kazon exploded a panel at the back of the bridge, but didn't make it through the shielding.

"You're breaking up! Stand by to transport!"

If *Voyager* transported now, the Kazon would dust this little ship like so much space debris, and all they'd have for their efforts was one less target to drawn the enemy's fire. *"Wait!"* He had their timing down now. Glaring powerfully through the splintering viewscreen, Chakotay waited until he saw the weapons tubes at the mouth of the vessel glow orange, then ducked his limping ship straight downward when it was too late for the Kazon to alter their lock. The shot went wild above him. That left a good six seconds before they could bring whatever cannon they were shooting back up to charge. Pumping the last of his ship's power into a leap he knew would probably rip its loyal engines apart, Chakotay spiraled toward the cruiser's wide-open belly and waited until nothing but starship filled his viewscreen, nothing but momentum still powered his craft.

"Now!"

The brilliance of destruction overwhelmed him, blasting away even the coarse *boom!* of impact and the undignified reality of pain. Then the spangles of triumphant light closed around him in a column of warm, welcome song, and lifted him away into nothing.

CHAPTER

21

A PEAL OF WHAT MIGHT HAVE BEEN SUMMER THUNDER trembled through the darkened barn, and Janeway found herself glancing upward in response. She wondered what was happening with the battle outside.

The holographic projection lifted its whiteless eyes to a point beyond Janeway's shoulder. Twisting around, she saw Tuvok approaching softly through the darkness, his tricorder now folded shut in one hand. "I can access the system to send us back to Federation space," he reported, squatting beside her, "but it will take several hours to activate."

Several hours the Kazon weren't likely to give

them. Janeway turned back to the entity with hand extended. "Unless you help us . . ."

It looked away, its face all but fading. "I wish I could. But I have very little time left." Lips moving, it stared blindly outward for several seconds before its voice abruptly returned. "I am taking your advice. I've begun to transmit the contents of my data banks to the Ocampa." It blinked, all attention coming back to them in a flash. "I have also initiated a self-destruct program."

Janeway's heart leapt into her throat. "If you destroy the Array, we'll have no way to get home!"

"The Ocampa's enemies cannot be allowed to control this installation," the entity whispered. She didn't know if she was hearing its voice, or simply reading the words off its fading lips. "In minutes, it will be destroyed." Its face loomed closer, and this time the voice came from nowhere specific that Janeway could name. *You have to go now.*

She thought at first that the entity had physically banished them, thrown them somewhere far from the Array with the same powerful abruptness with which it had seized their ships and stolen their bodies. Her body felt battered, plummeting down to nowhere, striking a hard surface that pitched and slewed beneath her like the deck of a dying ship. Then the darkness of the barn leapt back into existence, flickered away, dashed back again. Janeway pushed up onto her elbows, craning around for Tuvok. Cloudy, smoke-filled light suddenly became the final reality, and she recognized her security officer climbing to his knees a few meters away at the same time as she placed the huge, open room now around them as the same depthless chamber Kim and Paris had discovered on their first visit to the Array. Whatever had happened, it had eradicated whatever maintained the holographic projection system. Janeway didn't know if that was good or bad.

She rolled onto her back, slapping at her comm badge. *"Voyager,* report!"

"A Kazon vessel just collided with the Array, Captain. . . ." Paris's voice crackled and broke across the open channel. Behind him, Janeway could hear the battering *Voyager* must be taking. "Are you all right?"

"Affirmative." She took the hand Tuvok held out for her and pulled herself to her feet. "Stand by."

Where the entity's holographic projection had huddled only moments before, a huge, vaporous creature now heaved and groaned. *The termination program . . . has been . . . damaged . . .* It recoiled from Janeway's instinctive approach. *The Kazon . . . must not gain . . .* Something deep inside its fragile bulk seemed to flux against itself and shatter. *. . . control . . . of this installation . . .* Then it folded down with a heavy sigh, ever smaller, ever darker, until the last glimmer of its physical form misted completely away.

At Janeway's feet, a misshapen lump of what

looked like some alien ore twinkled weakly before slipping into total darkness. The captain wished she had time for a respectful farewell, not to mention some idea what the Caretaker would have considered appropriate. Instead, there was hardly even time left to save themselves.

Tuvok moved up alongside her. "Shall I activate the program to get us back?" he asked softly.

Janeway couldn't tear her eyes from the Caretaker's pitiful remains. "And what happens to the Ocampa after we're gone?"

She almost felt the jolt of alarm pass through the Vulcan's body. "Captain . . ." He stepped formally into her line of vision, capturing her full attention in the most expedient way available. "Any action we take to protect the Ocampa would affect the balance of power in this system. The Prime Directive," he emphasized, "would seem to apply."

"Would it?" If he were human, Janeway would have suspected him of invoking the Prime Directive in an effort to manipulate her decision. But Tuvok was a Vulcan, and one of the most honorable men of that race she had ever had the pleasure of knowing. He could only ever speak what he believed to be the truth.

"We never asked to be involved, Tuvok," she told him. "But we are." She sighed down at the twisted metal lump. "We are."

And running away wouldn't be the answer to that involvement, any more than calling on the Prime

Directive would help her to pretend their presence here hadn't already impacted with horrible consequences.

Smiling sadly in unspoken apology, she said simply, "I'm afraid your family will have to wait a little longer for you."

If any doubt stirred within that implacable Vulcan exterior, Janeway would never know. Tuvok nodded polite acknowledgment, then stooped gracefully to retrieve what was left of the entity who had cared for this system so tenderly for so long.

We won't let them down, Janeway promised. *We'll make sure you see this through.* She tapped her comm badge as Tuvok moved into position beside her. "Away team to *Voyager.* Two to transport."

Voyager bridge was positively crowded by the time Janeway and Tuvok arrived. When the turbolift released them, Janeway had to shoulder her way past both Torres and Chakotay to reach the main walkway, and Torres actually growled at her in protest. Chakotay smelled like the burned remains of a fuel depository, and soot caked his clothes and hair as thickly as pollen on a flower. Janeway could only imagine where he had just been.

Trotting down the steps to her command chair, she tried to ignore the energy beams still splattering like lightning strikes against their failing shields. "Mr. Tuvok, ready a tricobalt device."

"Aye, Captain."

Paris jerked around at the conn, but Janeway didn't have time to explain. "Open a channel to the Kazon," she ordered Kim.

He turned without question to his station. "Channel open."

The viewscreen rippled and re-formed, replacing the image of a damaged Array with Jabin's weather-beaten face. The Kazon leader wasted no time on empty pleasantries. "Be advised, Captain—I have called for additional ships."

Janeway couldn't help smiling a little at the pointlessness of that threat. "I'm calling to warn you to move your vessels to a safe distance. I intend to destroy the Array."

Jabin's face went still with shock. "You can't do that."

"I can," Janeway told him, "and I will." Not that she needed his permission. She tossed a nod at Kim. "End transmission."

Almost immediately, the ship rocked beneath a new torpedo strike. Janeway clung grimly to her chair as Kim announced needlessly, "They're increasing fire, Captain. Shields are holding."

At least something was working in their favor. "Move us four hundred kilometers from the Array, Mr. Paris."

"Yes, ma'am."

"What are you *doing?*" Torres lunged across the railing, almost into Janeway's lap. "That Array is the only way we have to get back home!"

Not enough time, the Caretaker had told them.

That warning became more and more true with every passing second. "I'm aware everyone has families and loved ones at home they want to get back to," Janeway explained as calmly and simply as possible. "So do I. But I'm not willing to trade the lives of the Ocampa for our . . . convenience." Dammit, they deserved better than this—they all deserved better than this. "We'll have to find another way home."

Torres barked angry laughter. *"What other way home is there?"* Chakotay grabbed her when she would have surged forward and blocked the view of the main screen. Janeway silently thanked him for his interference even as Torres whirled on him to snarl, "Who is she to be making these decisions for all of us?"

"She's the captain." He pulled her with him back onto the upper level, leaving the bridge open for the crew to do their duties.

He must have been a fine commander when Starfleet had him, Janeway thought. That was the Federation's loss.

Tuvok looked up from the tactical station. "The tricobalt device is ready."

"In position," Paris sang out from the conn.

Which left only one thing to be done, one thing to be said before there was no more turning back from what they had set into motion. Taking a deep breath, Janeway nodded stiffly. "Fire."

Voyager shuddered only faintly when the tricobalt device was released, a barely noticeable tremor compared to the battering she was already suffering from the Kazon fighters. A spinning glimmer of energy, flashing like a brilliant diamond, arced out from under the nose of the starship, speeding through the glowing sea of battle debris on its way toward the Array. One of the Kazon ships broke off its attack. Hoping to pursue the device, Janeway guessed, thinking it could stop the inevitable. What the Kazon thought didn't matter. As the deadly packet disappeared into the tangled strutwork of the Array, Janeway felt a whole universe of tension inside her uncoil and release with a throb of almost painful regret. *Over,* she greeted the blossom of destruction that boiled outward from the point of initial detonation. *It's all over now, nothing to be done. All over.* For the Caretaker, for the Ocampa, for all of them. The relief that came with no longer facing a decision surprised her, although perhaps it shouldn't have.

No one spoke for a very long time. At the rear of the bridge, Janeway could hear someone crying softly. She granted the person the privacy of not turning to see who it was.

"The lead Kazon ship is hailing us," Kim said after a long moment of listening to the incoming signal chirp at him.

It was too much to hope Jabin would simply leave them alone. "Onscreen."

As it was, the hatred blazing in the Kazon leader's eyes nearly drilled a hole through the starship's heart. "You have made an enemy today."

Then he cut the channel without giving her a chance to reply.

Not that she had anything to say.

Tuvok glanced up from his console, the only composed figure on the bridge. "They are withdrawing, Captain." For everyone else's benefit, Janeway assumed, as much as for hers.

On the viewscreen, an ever-expanding plasma cloud that used to be the Array swelled silently outward until it finally filled the night—obscuring, at least for the moment, all thought of life beyond itself, all hope of anything but the salvation it no longer offered.

CHAPTER
22

STEPPING INTO THE CAPTAIN'S READY ROOM, PARIS wasn't sure what to expect. To be keelhauled, maybe. Or at least dressed down for his sins.

The excitement of battle had swept over him with a frightening abandon. It had never been like this with the Maquis—he had never been invaded with such a sense of duty and purpose that he had said things, done things, that only a member of a starship's crew had any right to. And, greatest sin of all, he'd intentionally failed to inform Captain Janeway, "Hey, I'm a felon. Remember?" when she herself seemed to forget that fact in the thick of everything else. It had just felt so good to fit in again. So good to be useful.

Janeway turned away from the observation window as the door whispered shut behind Paris. He glimpsed a faint surprise in her eyes, as though she hadn't expected him so soon; then she stepped smoothly to the monitor on the long table between them and switched it off without looking at it. A suggestion of loneliness—a man's smiling face, and a blur of big, huggable dog—blinked out of existence before Paris even had a chance to blush at his intrusion.

"You asked to see me, Captain?" he prompted, just to break the moment.

She nodded, folding her hands. "Mr. Paris, you have a problem."

It occurred to him that the first time a woman had told him that was probably in fifth grade.

"I've invited Chakotay and the other Maquis to become part of this crew," Janeway went on. "It seemed the only reasonable thing to do, under the circumstances."

Paris swallowed an insane urge to giggle. "Will you provide a bodyguard for me, Captain?" It seemed somehow so unfair to be murdered in his sleep after surviving everything else they'd been through.

Janeway smiled oddly. "It seems you already have one."

"I do?"

"Mr. Chakotay said something about his life belonging to you?" She shook her head, obviously at a loss about how to take the reference, while

Paris allowed himself a thoroughly evil grin. "He'll be taking responsibility for your safety."

"I think I'm going to enjoy this," Paris admitted.

Janeway cocked her head in speculation. "Don't be so sure. He's also going to be my first officer. Everyone aboard this ship will report to him." She captured Paris's eyes with her own. "Including the lieutenant assigned to the conn."

At first, he was going to snort and ask what the hell this had to do with him. But something in his throat knotted before any sound came out, and his brain caught up an instant later. "Me?"

"I've entered into the ship's log on this date that I'm granting a field commission of lieutenant to Thomas Eugene Paris." She leaned across the table to offer him her hand and a welcoming smile. "Congratulations."

Paris wrapped her hand in both of his, shaking it with a gratefulness his heart didn't feel ready to contain. "For the first time in my life . . . I don't know what to say!"

He didn't even mean to it to be funny, but Janeway still smiled as she rounded the table to walk him toward the door. "You've earned this, Tom. I'm only sorry your father won't know."

It was the first time she'd spoken with anything approaching doubt. That subtle change in her demeanor startled Paris into an honesty he never could have mustered if he'd tried. "He'll know," he promised her. "When we get back." *Because if I can be standing here with your respect and a renewed commission, then I have to believe that anything is possible. Anything.*

Sometimes, it amazed Janeway how far a small amount of praise could go toward bolstering a young person's confidence. She wondered if it maybe wasn't so obvious to parents, who were often too entwined in their children's lives to have any real objectivity about what was going on. All she knew was that in the last few days, Tom Paris had somehow grown from an irresponsible child to a young adult any father would have been proud to raise. And contrary to what everyone had always feared about Paris, the loading of additional trust on his young shoulders had only pushed him that one step closer to true manhood. Janeway was looking forward to knowing him once he got there.

"Ah, Captain . . ." Neelix's voice warbled through the still-open doors just ahead of his and Kes's arrival. "We were just coming to see you."

Janeway stood again, smiling as the alien couple gaped around the empty ready room as though it were filled with endless wonders. Perhaps the sight of such clean, well-built technology was much the same thing to them. "We've supplied your ship with water, Neelix," she told him. "It's ready to go." It had seemed the least they could do after his and Kes's help in recovering their crew.

Neelix bobbed his bald head nervously, clinging to Kes's hand. "Well, you see . . . that's what we wanted to discuss. . . ." He took a deep breath and plowed ahead. "We'd like to go with you."

Janeway blinked at him. And here she thought the little alien had exhausted his ability to startle her. "I'm sorry—this isn't a passenger ship—"

"Of course not!" Kes jumped in. "We won't be passengers—"

"—we'll be valuable colleagues," Neelix added.

"Colleagues?" She probably shouldn't have spoken—the encouragement just seemed to fill him with more energy.

"Whatever you need," Neelix announced with Faginesque charm, "is what I have to offer. You need a guide? I'm your guide. You need supplies? I know where to procure them—I have friends among races you don't even know exist. You need a cook? You haven't *lived* until you've tasted my *angla'bosque.*" Janeway wasn't sure if it would even be possible to add something so exotic to the replicators, but decided not to mention that. "It will be my job to anticipate your needs before you know you have them," Neelix persisted. A puckish twinkle lit in his eye. "And I anticipate your first need will be—me!"

He was good. Janeway had to give him that.

"And where I go—" Neelix pulled Kes into a possessive embrace. "—she goes."

"In my own way," Kes said, as though wanting to make sure Janeway understood that this was *her* decision, too, "I'm an explorer, Captain. On my world, exploration meant defying the Caretaker just to walk on the surface. I took that chance because I had to. My father taught me that the greatest thing an Ocampa can do is to open her mind to all the experiences and challenges that life has to offer." She looked around the room that Janeway found so familiar and unromantic, and the look of naked wonder on the Ocampa's face was heartbreaking. "I can't begin to imagine where this ship might take us! I know I'll never see my homeworld again. But I want very much to be part of your journey."

Janeway studied her in gentle amazement. How could anyone say no to someone who instinctively understood the heart of Starfleet so well? She nodded acceptance, and knew right away it was the right thing to do.

Sighing, Neelix hugged Kes to him ever tighter and smiled up at Janeway in sincerest bliss. "Isn't she *remarkable?*"

Yes, Janeway thought in wonder. *Aren't we all?*

The bridge was still crowded, but in a calmer, less claustrophobic way. Most of the debris had been removed since the Kazon battle, and at least half the panels were functioning again. The rest were patched closed. Janeway hadn't even begun to think about where they would get replacement parts, or even enough repair crews, and being faced with the hint that it would all have to be dealt with soon made her head hurt.

What have I gotten us into?

Chakotay waited at the first officer's station,

wearing his new Starfleet uniform as though he'd never taken it off. At engineering, Torres only looked a little uncomfortable in her corresponding gold-and-black, but Janeway still thought it best to encourage crew unity in every way possible, especially at the beginning. If that meant squeezing Maquis into uniforms they didn't wear easily, then it was just one of many adjustments they were all going to have to make.

She stepped down to her command chair, and tried to touch each expectant look with a reassuring nod. On the viewscreen, Kes's homeworld drifted lazily, an unchanging marble of dusty amber.

"We're alone in an uncharted part of the galaxy." It seemed best to start with the things they all knew—the obvious things that were already half-digested. "We've already made some friends here," she went on, nodding toward Kes and Neelix near the turbolifts, "and some enemies." The destruction still plaguing most levels of the ship spoke eloquently enough about that. "We have no idea of the dangers we're going to face. But one thing is clear—both crews are going to have to work together if we're to survive. That's why Commander Chakotay and I have agreed that this should be *one* crew. A Starfleet crew."

She saw Torres tug at the front of her uniform in evident distaste, but pretended not to notice. There would be time to iron out all the crew's behavioral wrinkles later.

"And as the only Starfleet vessel 'assigned' to the

Delta Quadrant, we'll continue to follow our directive to seek out new worlds and explore space."

She moved toward the front of the bridge, so she could face them all without turning. Did she have any real reason to hope that this disparate bunch could ever bond and become a real working unit? And what could she do about it if they didn't? Their future together was likely to be longer than any of them wanted.

Janeway shook such thoughts away for the time being and focused instead on their more immediate situation. "Our primary goal is clear. Even at maximum speeds, it would take seventy-five years to reach the Federation." She shook her head at their looks of dismay. "I'm not willing to settle for that. There's another entity like the Caretaker out there somewhere who has the ability to get us there a lot faster. We'll be looking for her. And we'll be looking for wormholes, spatial rifts, or new technologies to help us. Somewhere along this journey," she promised with everything that was in her, "we'll find a way back."

Turning, she rested her hands on the back of Paris's chair, and looked beyond his head at the eternal possibilities waiting for them behind every planet, every star. "Mr. Paris, set a course . . ." She tried to say it with enough conviction and faith for all of them. ". . . for home."

It was likely to be a very long trip. But if heart and hope and bravery could lead them, she knew they would make it. All they would need was time.

About the Authors

L. A. Graf is the pen name used by authors Julia Ecklar and Karen Rose Cercone for six popular novels since 1992, including the *Star Trek: The Lost Years* novel *Traitor Winds* and the upcoming *Alien Nation* novel *Extreme Prejudice.*

Julia Ecklar is an award-winning science-fiction writer whose latest novel, *ReGenesis,* will be available from Ace Science Fiction in June 1995. This novel, based on the popular Rahel Tovin stories first published in *Analog* magazine, deals with issues of extinction and genetic re-creation in the far future. These and other stories won her the John W. Campbell Award for Best New Science Fiction Writer of the Year in 1991. As the macho, athletic one of the pair, she's responsible for most of the explosions and hand-to-hand combat.

Karen Rose Cercone is the university scientist of the pair, with a doctorate in geochemistry and a professorship at Indiana University of Pennsylvania, where she teaches environmental geoscience and science fiction. In a natural division of labor, she gets to be in charge of creating strange planetary environments for all of L. A. Graf's books.

As well as planning to branch out into original science fiction as L. A. Graf, the two authors are currently hoping to wreak some havoc on DS9 in their next collaboration.

1252.01